# SALOME

# SALOME

Beatrice Gormley

ALFRED A. KNOPF
NEW YORK

I would like to thank Jordan Rosenblum, the scholar of ancient Judaism who read and commented on *Salome* in manuscript. I also thank Professor Kathleen O'Connor of Columbia Theological Seminary and the Rev. Dr. J. Gregory Prior of St. Andrew's, Little Compton, Rhode Island, for their advice and inspiration.

THIS IS A BORZOI BOOK PUBLISHED BY ALFRED A. KNOPF

www.randomhouse.com/teens

Educators and librarians, for a variety of teaching tools, visit us at
www.randomhouse.com/teachers

Library of Congress Cataloging-in-Publication Data
Gormley, Beatrice.
Salome / by Beatrice Gormley. — 1st ed.
p. cm.
SUMMARY: Relates the life of a beautiful descendant of Herod the Great, and events leading up to her Dance of the Seven Veils, after which her cruel mother coerces her to ask for the head of John the Baptist, an innocent man, on a silver platter.
ISBN 978-0-375-83908-5 (trade) — ISBN 978-0-375-93908-2 (lib. bdg.)
1. Salome (Biblical figure)—Juvenile fiction. [1. Salome (Biblical figure)—Fiction. 2. Herodias—Fiction. 3. Herod Antipas, Tetrarch of Galilee—Fiction. 4. Dance—Fiction. 5. Bible N.T.—History of Biblical events—Fiction. 6. Rome—History—Empire, 30 B.C.–284 A.D.—Fiction.] I. Title.
PZ7.G6696Sal 2007
[Fic]—dc22
2006029197

Printed in the United States of America

April 2007

10 9 8 7 6 5 4 3 2 1

First Edition

*To my agent, Susan Cohen*

# CONTENTS

# SALOME'S FAMILY TREE

HEROD THE GREAT    *married*   DORIS

                        *married*   MARIAMNE I

                        *married*   MARIAMNE II

                        *married*   MALTHACE

                        *married*   CLEOPATRA OF JERUSALEM

ANTIPATER

ARISTOBULUS *married* BERNICE
ALEXANDER

HEROD JUNIOR *married* HERODIAS (1ST *marriage*)

ANTIPAS *married* HERODIAS (2ND *marriage*)
ARCHELAUS

PHILIP

AGRIPPA
HERODIAS

SALOME

# SALOME SPEAKS

If I'd never hoped to live in a world of goodness and truth—if the priestess of Diana, then Leander, and then Joanna hadn't shown me glimpses of it—maybe I wouldn't have minded being shut out of it. Maybe the preacher's death wouldn't have trapped me in a dungeon, the dungeon of my own self.

Have you ever seen a dungeon? This is what it would be like if you visited the dungeon beneath Herod Antipas's palace in Tiberias. First the prison door thuds behind you. A guard walks you down the corridor. His torch shows rough stone walls on either side, stone underfoot, stone overhead.

Stone steps lead down to the lowest level. It's cold

underground, but not too cold to smell the stink from the cells. Past the last cell, steps lead down again, and there's an iron grate in the floor. The grate covers a hole in the rock. A deep hole, like a well. Only instead of water, this well is full of despair.

I put myself in the well of despair.

How could this be, that I came to choose death-in-life? I'm not sure I know how it happened myself. But one thing you have to understand: Herodias and I were best friends before *he* came along. Or I thought we were.

("You have to understand," I say. Of course, I don't have any special right to be understood. Neither does Herodias, although she often uses those words, as if everyone should understand her—everyone should sympathize with her.)

My mother, Herodias, was more like an older sister than a mother to me. She'd been only thirteen when she married my father, Herod. "Herod of Rome," he was called, to set him apart from his late father, King Herod of Judea. His friends called him "Junior." He was much older than my mother—in fact, he was one of her uncles.

Growing up in Rome, I knew my father as the paunchy man who left our house early in the morning and came home after I was in bed. When he was home, he was usually in the dining hall with friends. I overheard bits of their talk about the chariot races or about which officer the Emperor was supposed to appoint to some post or other.

Those dinner parties sounded as dull as dust to me, but my mother managed to get a great deal of fun out of them. Instead of listening to the talk, she'd notice how my father always leaned forward with his eyes wide and forefinger jabbing to make a point. Or how his friend Secundus would answer, "Well, well," no matter what was said and give a series of burps. Later Herodias would amuse me and my nursemaid, Gundi, by imitating my father and his guests. Her light, musical laugh could cut anyone down to size. It was reassuring to me, because I was a little afraid of the men, including my father.

Sometimes at night I overheard my parents quarreling. It often started when my father accused Herodias of throwing away his money on her spendthrift brother Agrippa. Herodias then called my father a skinflint to his family who threw *his* money away on his racetrack friends. My father called *her* a poor excuse for a wife, producing only one girl (me) in all these years. Herodias asked why he needed a son and heir, since he hadn't become king of Judea after all. At this point Gundi would give me lambs' wool to stop up my ears, but she stood at the door to listen.

I never called Herodias "Mama"; she was always

"Herodias" to me. When I was little, I called Gundi "Mama," but I grew out of that. Herodias and I laughed at my childish mistake. The idea that my nursemaid, Gundi, a slave from a northern land, with her ruddy face and harsh accent, could be the mother of Salome, descended from the royal Herodian line!

So I was a girl without a "Mama." But I thought I was lucky, because I lived with the most wonderful friend.

When Herodias was around, everything was fun and treats. Gundi did the dull, unpleasant things with me, like combing the snarls out of my hair and correcting my manners. She tried to get me to stop twirling a lock of my hair, a habit I fell into when I was anxious. "After all my trouble to groom your hair, Miss Salome!"

Sometimes, when I missed my mother, I would hit out at Gundi. She held my wrists and made reproachful clucking noises, but she couldn't punish me. She was, after all, a slave.

Returning home from a shopping trip, Herodias would call my name as she stepped into the atrium. I came running to see what little gifts she'd brought me from the market—fresh dates, maybe, or a trinket—but the real gift was the way she drew me into a charmed circle just for the two of us.

When she was home, Herodias played clapping games

with me and sang me songs. After Gundi had put me to bed, she would come to my room and give me a sip of honeyed wine from her own goblet. "Sleep well, my dearest pet." I worshiped Herodias more sincerely than I worshiped any god. For the longest time I had faith—a faith so deep that I didn't even know I believed it—that I would grow closer and closer to my mother as I grew up. If I was worthy, the two of us would become inseparable.

As I grew older, Herodias did spend more time with me. She took me on outings to the theater, picnics on the Tiber River, holiday trips to a resort on Lake Sabazia. I only wished these events didn't include other people, often relatives visiting Rome from other parts of the Empire.

Herodias didn't have close women friends, but she delighted in giving parties for other ladies and their children. It was a good excuse for her to show off her talents. Like most women, Herodias hadn't had much education, but she had an excellent memory. She loved to read poetry and novels, and she could recite many long poems by heart.

Sometimes I would ask Gundi, "Do you think I will be as pretty as Herodias when I grow up?" or, "Do you think I will be as clever as Herodias?" I didn't mean that I wanted to rival my mother—only that I wanted to be worthy of her love.

Gundi wouldn't answer these questions, except to say, "What nonsense," or, "Clever is as clever does." I was afraid her answers really meant no, there was no chance that I would deserve to dwell in the charmed circle with Herodias forever.

# ONE

# UNCLE ANTIPAS

Ordinarily, upper-class Roman girls didn't dance. Dancers were lower-class entertainers, sluts. But it was entirely proper for well-bred girls to dance in the rites at the Temple of Diana. Diana, goddess of the moon and of the hunt, was also the protector of young girls. So, many well-to-do families sent their daughters for lessons at the Temple. There we received training in deportment (which is what our mothers cared about) and got to run around with other girls (which is what we cared about).

We Herods weren't actually Roman, of course: we were Jews from Judea. But like other wealthy foreigners in Rome—no matter whether they were from Ephesus in Anatolia,

Cyrene in Africa, or Gadis in Spain—we lived an upper-class Roman life. There were many Jews of lesser birth in Rome, but for the most part they kept to themselves in the Jewish quarter of the city. Their women hardly went out at all.

By the time I was twelve, I looked forward even more than before to my lessons at the Temple of Diana. I'd been enrolled at the Temple for years, and I'd always liked the training, especially learning the sacred songs and dances. The priestess was strict but kind to all the girls, and there was a peaceful sense of order in the Temple grounds.

Now I grew quickly, and soon I was tall for my age. My size made me feel awkward, and I had to struggle to make my hands and feet do what they were supposed to. Herodias joked that I would cross a room in order to find the one loose floor tile and stumble over it.

Since I felt so clumsy, I was grateful that I could dance as well as ever. Even with my new self-consciousness, I could still move gracefully when the pipes and tambourines started up. The music seemed to guide my body for me. I danced well even on festival days, when all the mothers came to the Temple to watch us take part in the rites.

One afternoon in November when I was just fourteen, I hurried home from the Temple, accompanied as usual by

Gundi. I was glowing with pride. Today the priestess had taken me aside and spoken to me. She'd been watching my progress, and she wondered if I might have a calling to become a priestess.

"I am going to recommend that you try for a sign from Diana this spring," she said. "One night during a full moon, you will sleep in the Temple at the feet of the great statue. If the goddess chooses you to serve her, she will give some sign." She would talk to my mother about it and consult the auspices for a favorable date.

I was flattered, although I hadn't thought of joining the cult. I knew that my mother's only purpose in sending me to the Temple of Diana was to help me gain poise and a proper sense of my role as a woman of noble birth. Herodias liked to celebrate all kinds of holidays, but otherwise she wasn't very devout to any deities, including the Jewish god.

At home I brushed past the doorkeeper, eager to tell Herodias how the priestess had complimented me. Then I stopped short, seeing the atrium full of men. Most of them were dressed in Eastern robes, although a few husky fellows wore uniforms—short tunics and capes and leather breastplates. These guards were throwing dice. The other men talked among themselves, except for a young man in a long

Greek-style tunic and draped cloak. Leaning against a pillar, he was absorbed in reading a scroll.

"What's all this?" muttered Gundi. She took me by the elbow to hurry me away from the eyes of so many strange men. I supposed they must be the attendants of someone visiting my father. But my father was usually out, in the Forum, at this hour.

Pausing in the doorway to the garden, I saw Herodias sitting by the fountain. It was a pleasantly warm day, although the afternoons were short this time of year. There was a table beside her with wine and cakes.

"Salome, there you are," said Herodias. "Come greet your uncle Antipas." On a bench facing my mother, his back to me, sat a man in an embroidered robe.

I hadn't seen Antipas (actually Herodias's uncle and my great-uncle) for years. That time, he'd been visiting Rome with one of his half brothers, Philip of Gaulanitis. But I remembered his powerful neck and shoulders. Herod Antipas, ruler of Galilee and Perea on the eastern side of the Empire. Like my father, Herod Junior, Antipas was one of the many sons of the late King Herod the Great of Judea. It seemed these two half brothers were on speaking terms for the moment—you never could tell with the Herods.

I came into the garden and stood beside Herodias.

Antipas's iron gray hair was short in the Roman style, and his trimmed beard set off a rather delicate mouth. I said politely, "Welcome to Rome and to our house, Great-Uncle." I hoped he wouldn't be staying with us.

Taking a sip from his goblet, Antipas looked me over. He remarked to my mother, "She's grown, hasn't she? Salome doesn't look much like you, except for her big brown eyes."

Uncomfortable, I turned my big brown eyes aside to the mosaic on the fountain wall. It pictured a maenad, an attendant of the god Dionysus, whirling in an ecstatic dance.

Herodias patted my arm. "Yes, she reminds me of a calf—a dear sweet calf."

They went on with their conversation, mainly Herodias listening with rapt attention while Antipas talked. He had a deep, rich voice, and it grew warmer as he described Galilee. Herodias knew Jerusalem in Judea from her girlhood, but she'd hardly ever been to Galilee.

Antipas had hired a Roman city planner and built himself a beautiful capital city, named Tiberias in honor of the Emperor. This new city, on a slope above a lake (renamed Lake Tiberias in honor of the Emperor), was gifted with all the best features of Rome: a forum, a theater, a stadium. The public baths were especially luxurious, because of the natural hot springs.

And the palace! Antipas made a sweeping gesture, indicating a building grander than we could imagine. (I noticed how small his hands were in contrast with his thick body.) Whitest marble, the palace was, its roof covered with gold leaf.

Herodias seemed entranced with all these details. She kept her long-lashed dark eyes fixed on this half brother of her husband. Meanwhile, I watched her. Herodias was a slim, sleek woman, younger-seeming than her thirty-four years. I'd always thought she was beautiful, but I'd never seen a man gaze at her the way Antipas was doing. Antipas and Herodias almost seemed to be alone together. In a charmed circle.

As Antipas talked on about his building program for Tiberias, I fidgeted with the waist cord of my *stola*. My mother turned to me as if she'd forgotten I was standing there. "You may go, Salome dear." Antipas's eyes rested on me again for a moment.

His look made my insides tighten, and I forgot how to move. I swear the table with the wine pitcher was not in my way when I came into the garden, but somehow I bumped against it as I turned to leave. Herodias caught the pitcher before it fell off the table and broke, but the red liquid splashed over the tiles.

A maid rushed to mop up the spilled wine. Herodias joked

to Antipas, "Didn't I say Salome was like a calf?" Somehow I got out of the garden, my face burning.

I sulked in my room until Antipas left, and my mother found us there. Gundi was sorting out the clothes that were too small for me now while I sat on the bed, twirling a lock of my hair.

"Uncle Antipas is quite a man, isn't he?" said Herodias. "I never really noticed that before. He reminds me of a bull."

"I thought he looked more like a boar," I said, "with his thick head and body and small hands and feet." I was just being difficult; I knew what she meant. It was the way Antipas acted rather than the way he looked. The bull is in charge of the herd, and the other cattle know it. If the lesser cattle challenged him, he'd gore them with his horns.

"Look, Lady Herodias," said Gundi, "how your daughter's grown between her thirteenth and fourteenth birthdays."

"Why, Salome—you're almost as tall as I am." My mother turned her dimpled smile on me. "How could you grow up without telling me?"

Then my bad mood melted away, and I told Herodias what the priestess of Diana had said today. She praised me and kissed me, and I felt the enchanted circle snug around the two of us again.

"Of course you are a gifted dancer," said Herodias. "But

the Temple can't steal my dearest friend away from me, even to serve the goddess! No—I won't allow it." She winked mischievously. "No harm in going through the motions, though, to keep the priestess of Diana happy. It'll be an adventure for you to stay at the Temple one night."

When Herodias left the room, Gundi made a sort of snort, *"Hmph."* I ignored her. Gundi had known me ever since I was a baby, but she could never enter the charmed circle. She didn't understand my mother and me.

Holding another tunic up to my shoulders, Gundi paused. "My, my. You're getting to look more like sixteen than fourteen. You care about your Gundi, dear Miss Salome, don't you?"

This question seemed like a sudden change of subject, and I looked at her in surprise. "Of course I do."

"Then give a thought to your old nursemaid when they marry you off. Ask to have me included in your dowry."

Marry me off? Her words opened a door that I'd managed to keep shut until this moment. Some of my friends in the class at the Temple were already betrothed. I'd heard their mothers ask my mother what the family's plans were for me. Although she answered vaguely, she and my father must be thinking about a match.

Of course I would have to marry and leave Herodias,

but that change had always seemed too far in the future to worry about. Now it was in the near future, and I shrank back from it.

Only two days after his first visit, Uncle Antipas was back at our door. In the weeks to come, Herodias spent more and more time with him and less and less time with me. Each time he arrived, Antipas would ask for his brother, but my father was almost always out—at the baths, in the Forum, at the chariot races.

It occurred to me that my father didn't really want to see Antipas any more than Antipas really wanted to see Herod Junior. The two men didn't have much in common. To start, they'd been born to different mothers. Herod Junior's mother had been the daughter of the High Priest of Jerusalem, while Antipas's mother was a Samaritan noblewoman.

Worse, there was the matter of the inheritance. Before their father, old King Herod of Greater Judea, had died, Herod Junior was second in line to take the throne. Instead, Herod's last will had divided his kingdom among three other sons: Archelaus, Philip, and Antipas.

I couldn't see what Herodias had in common with Antipas, either, but she continued to be entranced with him. These days, even when my mother spent time with me, she spent most of it talking about Antipas and his wonderful city, Tiberias. "Antipas is the *only* Herod brother who understands how to live in the grand style," she said.

"Father certainly doesn't," I agreed. Herodias laughed and rolled her eyes; my father's disappointing way of life went without saying.

"But aside from Junior," she went on, "there's Philip—do you remember Uncle Philip of Gaulanitis? He never even travels to Rome anymore because of the expense. Imagine, a client ruler going for years and years without visiting the Imperial City! Instead, Antipas says, Philip spends all his time traveling around his pathetic little realm—letting his subjects pester him with their concerns! How does he expect to keep his subjects in awe if he hobnobs with them?"

Antipas, on the other hand, understood how to impress his subjects with showy ceremonies and fabulous banquets. He'd persuaded one of Rome's finest cooks to join his court. Apparently, this cook's baked fish was famous among the nobility all around the Mediterranean Sea.

"But Antipas's wife refuses to eat fish—can you imagine?" My mother giggled. "She's from a desert kingdom, Nabatea. It was a purely political marriage."

I disliked my uncle for taking my mother's company away, but beyond that, he made me nervous. Not that he paid much attention to me—he was all taken up with Herodias. But when he did notice me, I felt that he paid too much attention to me, just for a moment. The feeling was hard to explain even to myself. I certainly didn't try to explain it to anyone else.

Many times that winter Antipas escorted Herodias to the theater, and often they took me along. Why not?—they had a whole train with them already. There were Antipas's bodyguards and courtiers and secretary, and slaves carrying drinks and snacks and cushions, and of course Antipas's personal food taster. I suppose there were many people who would have liked to poison him. I almost wished they would.

The youngest courtier was Simon, a son of one of Antipas's many half sisters. He was related to me, too, distantly. I thought Simon was ridiculous, the way he dropped names of powerful people in Rome—even that of Sejanus, the Emperor's regent. Simon seemed to think that he was being groomed for an important position in the Empire. At every opportunity he spoke up, trying to sound experienced and knowledgeable. Other times he would strike a noble pose, as if a sculptor were working on a statue of him.

At the theater I sometimes ignored what was happening onstage and watched Antipas's Greek secretary, a young man named Leander. He always carried a scroll, a note tablet, and a stylus in the folds of his draped pallium, or cloak. He had deep-set hazel eyes and curly brown hair, tied back with a headband, and he spoke with a cultured accent. Herodias said he was from Alexandria, across the sea in Egypt, where he'd studied with some important philosopher. (This was one of Herodias's examples of how Antipas was willing to spend money to get the best of everything. My father, in contrast, was so stingy that he didn't even keep a scribe but hired one from the library at the public baths.)

Now and then Antipas would call Leander to his side and order him to come up with a fitting quotation from a Greek philosopher or to note down some insightful remark that Antipas had just made. Leander waited courteously on his master, but I thought it must be hard on an educated man to work as a mere secretary. Antipas seemed to enjoy keeping a pet philosopher at his beck and call, like a hunting dog. Herodias laughingly called Leander "our Socrates."

One time we went to see a Greek tragedy, but hardly anyone liked it. Antipas dozed off, his attendants whiled away the time by eating bunches of grapes and spitting out the seeds, and Herodias sighed through the long speeches. Antipas, awakening to one of her sighs, patted her hand. "A bit tedious, hmm? At my theater in Tiberias, they perform nothing but comedies."

Only Leander seemed intent on the play, mouthing the words along with the actors. At the end, all the characters were either dead or wished they were dead.

What I remembered most about that tragedy, long afterward, was the masks. After the play, the chief actor came out front to talk with Antipas, his patron. He took his mask off and set it on the edge of the stage, where it seemed to stare at me. The mouth was open, wrenched down at the corners. The eyes, too, were wide open in agony.

# TWO

# AT THE JORDAN RIVER

Far across the Mediterranean Sea from Rome, in the Jordan River Valley a few miles from Jericho, a different audience listened to a different speaker. The preacher's brown hair and beard were long and wild. His tunic, stitched together from old grain sacks, was belted around his gaunt body with rawhide.

"Brothers and sisters"—John's voice rang out over the crowd—"I have lived in the wilderness long years, waiting for the Lord's word to come to me. Now I bring you his message: Make a highway for the Lord!"

Here, where a creek flowed into the Jordan, the riverbank formed a natural amphitheater. John's listeners covered the slopes, crouching on the grass or leaning against sycamore trees. These people had little time to spare from scratching out a living, but still they were here. They were the women who hauled water from the village well to their homes every day, who might sell a few cheap clay cups in the market and then buy enough grain to feed their children one more week. They were the men who gathered at the city gates before dawn, hoping to be hired by a landowner for a day's work in his vineyards.

Pacing a flat boulder, his platform, John went on, "How do we make a highway? The prophet Isaiah says, 'Every valley shall be lifted up, and every mountain and hill be made low.' This is how we will make a highway—*for the Lord.*"

"A highway for the Lord," the crowd murmured. They understood exactly what John was *not* saying: a highway for the Lord instead of for the hated Romans. Most of these men had been grabbed by a Roman soldier at some time or other and forced to fill in a ravine or scrape off the top of a hill for one of the Empire's fine level roads, graded, paved, and clearly marked with milestones. Most of these women had trudged through the brush alongside a Roman highway. Peasants had to labor on road crews, but they were not allowed to walk on the Imperial roads.

At the sight of so many people drinking in his words,

John's heart swelled. He would have obeyed the Lord's calling whether anyone listened to him or not, but it was a great
joy to see how they listened. This was what he'd been born
for—to draw the people back to the Lord.

In a corner of his mind, John was aware of the Roman
soldier standing above the crowd, his crested helmet silhou-
etted against the sky. Elias, one of John's disciples, kept casting him wary glances. But the soldier wasn't listening to the
preacher, John knew; he probably didn't even understand
the Aramaic John spoke. The soldier's job was to watch the
audience. If the crowd got unruly, he'd signal for backup
troops.

The first time John's voice had boomed out over a crowd
like this, he'd been startled. In the wilderness with the lizards
and ravens, he'd gone for weeks without speaking at all. But
now, letting his voice resound felt as natural as breathing. It
was the Lord's message, not John's. It was the Lord's power.

"The Lord loves righteousness and justice!" John told his
listeners. That was a quotation from a psalm written generations ago, but it was still true. It would always be true.

"Yes!" shouted a man in the crowd. "Give us justice!"
Hundreds of hopeful faces looked up to John.

"In our land," John went on, "there is a ruler who calls
himself a Jew but lives like a Roman. He presumes to rule the

Lord's people—but he defiles the Law. He builds his city of marble and gold—on a Jewish graveyard. The Jews of Galilee can hardly find a place to live, but Antipas peoples his new city with foreigners. He raises graven images in the public square."

"Unclean," muttered John's audience. "Filthy pagan." They knew exactly what kind of "graven images" John was talking about. The worst was the statue of the previous Roman emperor, the "divine" Augustus Caesar.

The same man who'd spoken up before shouted, "Herod Antipas eats swine flesh!"

"The Herods have Jewish blood on their hands," John went on. "Antipas's father called himself Herod the Great. Great—yes, at squeezing taxes from the farmers and fishermen in order to clothe himself in gold. Great at hunting down and butchering the righteous Jews who rose against him. Every luxurious palace of his, like the one at Macherus"—he waved a hand eastward—"squats on top of dungeons and torture chambers."

John's audience knew the grisly stories about Herod the Great, and most of them had some personal connection with them. One of John's own cousins had barely escaped being slaughtered at birth by Herod's soldiers. Alarmed by a rumor that the new king of the Jews had been born in Bethlehem,

King Herod ordered all the male babies in that town to be killed. To be on the safe side, his soldiers had massacred all the boys under two years of age.

"Woe to the tyrants!" shouted the man who'd spoken before. Judging by his rough clothing and weathered face, he was probably a shepherd. It wasn't surprising that most of the crowd were humble folk—shepherds, farmers, poor craftsmen. It was the ordinary people who were crushed by injustice.

What was surprising was the number of well-dressed people among the peasants. John noticed two men in scribes' robes in a comfortable spot under an oak tree. And there, at the edge of the pool formed by the creek, a wealthy woman leaned out of a litter. The scribes must be keeping an eye on John for the High Priest in Jerusalem. The woman was curious, no doubt. Well, he had a message for all of them.

"Brothers and sisters," cried John. "This is what the Lord commanded me: *Call the people to repent. Tell them the kingdom of heaven is at hand. When they repent, baptize them.*" His voice rang over the water like a trumpet. "Do you want to be right with the Lord? Hear what he asks of you. Repent! Turn from your sins! As the psalm says, 'It is time for the Lord to act, for your law has been broken.' "

"I repent!" responded a chorus of voices. "Lord, save us!"

When John had finished preaching, he felt shaky and

spent. He climbed down from the boulder to get out of the sun. As he waded toward the riverbank, a man splashed into the river, holding up the hem of his fine coat. "Rabbi!"

The people near him drew back, and one woman spat at him. "Filthy tax collector!"

The tax collector ignored everyone but John. "Rabbi— how can I repent?" His plump chin quivered.

Elias looked at John as if expecting a signal to push the tax collector away, but John waited for the man to come closer. "Lord," he murmured, "you want to save all your people." He was deeply moved, and his eyes stung. How hungry even the tax collectors were for the word of the Lord! "Don't collect any more than the legal rate," he told the man. "If you've cheated anyone, pay them back."

The woman who'd spat at the tax collector gave a short, sour laugh. But the man, keeping his eyes on John, nodded humbly. "When you've lived in repentance for a month," John went on, "you'll be clean inside. Then come back here to be washed clean outside."

John started to wade forward again, but another man called out in a Syrian accent, "Rabbi, wait!" The wealthy woman's litter swung around to meet him. The nearest of the four litter bearers went on, "Rabbi, can I ask you a question? My lady wants to know what she should do to repent."

Elias stepped in front of John, indignant that his tired master was being bothered. "Carry that litter away from here!" he told the servant. "The Rabbi has taken a vow not to speak to women. Besides—aren't you from the accursed household of Herod Antipas?"

John held up his hand. "Tell your mistress to share her riches with the poor," he said to the litter bearer. "This will be pleasing to the Lord." Elias was right: the Tetrarch's insignia adorned the roof of the litter. But that was all the more miraculous, that the word of the Lord could reach into Antipas's own household.

# THREE

# A SURPRISE PERFORMANCE

In Rome the winter wore on, cold and rainy. "How much longer will Uncle Antipas stay here?" I asked Herodias. "Isn't it hard to rule Galilee and Perea from so far away?"

"He can't go back there now because there's no sailing on the Mediterranean until spring, silly," said my mother. "And Antipas has a trusted steward in Galilee to mind his affairs. Steward Chuza sends him reports. Very detailed reports, in fact." She rolled her eyes. "Chuza tells Antipas *exactly* how many stonemasons he hired to enlarge his prisons and *exactly* how he calculated the extra amount to tax the peasants in order to pay the stonemasons. Oh, such details!"

Putting on an earnest expression, Herodias pretended to

read from a tablet. "To my prince Herod Antipas, greetings. Some insignificant rabble-rousers from the hill country have been arrested and brought in for questioning. The *tediously* complete record of the interrogation is enclosed. Oh, and furthermore, my prince, the donkeys' groom's boy stubbed his toe yesterday. . . ."

January and February passed. At the Temple of Diana, the priestess paid special attention to me. The other girls found out that I was to ask the goddess about a calling, and they gave me respectful looks. (I didn't explain that my mother was only pretending to let me try for a calling.) But Herodias seemed to notice me less and less—when she was home at all, for she was often gone with Antipas.

One wet morning in March, Herodias and Antipas were in the reception room playing a board game. They might be there for hours, I knew. Gundi was in the kitchen, gossiping with Herodias's maid, Iris.

I wandered into the atrium, where rainwater trickled from the open roof into the pool. I was not supposed to be in the public parts of the house without Gundi, but no one was paying any attention. Besides, I thought, Herodias herself wasn't behaving in such a seemly way for a married woman. Why should I worry about being proper?

Antipas's attendants chatted or tossed dice, as usual. All

the attendants, that is, except for Leander, the secretary. The Greek sat hunched on a bench by himself, leaning away from the splashing water as he read a scroll.

What could be in the scroll to make him forget everything around him? "What are you reading, secretary?"

Startled, Leander looked up. His deep-set eyes focused on me as I sat down on the other end of the bench. He half got up, as if I were a lady, then seemed to decide that I was a child and sat down again. It made me smile, it was so clear what was going through his mind.

"I'm reading Plato, miss. About the death of Socrates in Athens. Socrates was a—" He frowned, seeming to wonder if maybe I was a young lady after all. "Shouldn't your chaperone be with you?"

It was fun, teasing the Greek a little. I shrugged, as if to say I didn't really need a chaperone. "Yes, but I didn't want to bother her. Are you from Athens?"

No, answered Leander, he was from Alexandria, in Egypt, where many Greeks had settled. "If it weren't for my dying father's request, I'd still be in Alexandria." A note of homesickness crept into his voice as he stared into the gloomy corners of the atrium. "The sun would be shining. . . . I'd be sitting in the courtyard of the *gymnasion,* arguing with the other students, or we'd be listening to our teacher. . . ."

"What was your dying father's request?" I asked. This was the most interesting conversation I'd had with anyone for months.

But Leander glanced uneasily at the courtiers on the other side of the pool. "Really, miss—" He stood up and bowed. "I am sure your chaperone is looking for you."

I didn't want to worry him too much, and I knew he'd be blamed if Herodias saw us talking alone. But then I thought of something important he could answer for me. "Just one more question—please?" I stood up, too, clasping my hands. "Do you know how much longer Uncle Antipas will stay in Rome?"

Leander looked surprised that I seemed to care so much. "How much longer? Well, the winter's more or less over, and the Tetrarch's business here is almost done. He's waiting mainly for the ship he hired to be refitted. It's a cargo ship, meant to transport grain. So they're building cabins on it, and then they'll stock it with supplies for all of us." He nodded around the atrium at the guards and courtiers. "That'll take another week or so, I suppose."

What good news! "Thank you." Giving him a big smile, I skipped out of the atrium.

Only a week or so and Antipas would be gone! Then Herodias would spend time with me again. I'd share all the little things I'd been saving up to tell her, and she'd do an imitation of Antipas to make me laugh. The charmed circle would close around the two of us again.

I expected that since Antipas was leaving Rome so soon, my mother would want to spend every moment with him. To my surprise, that very day she began to plan one of her elaborate drama afternoons.

"Our last production, on my birthday, was such a great success," said Herodias. She beamed at me. "The ladies said you danced like a nymph."

I felt warm with pride, but I said modestly, "Of course they liked the story of Demeter and Persephone. They're all mothers." The heroine of that myth is the devoted mother Demeter, goddess of grain and the harvest. Demeter is heartbroken when her daughter, Persephone, is stolen away by Pluto, god of the underworld.

Acting out the myth, Herodias played the part of Demeter, wearing a *stola* as blue as the summer sky. She had me play the part of Persephone, while Gundi, wearing a black cloak and a frightening mask, played Pluto. Iris and the other servants stood in back by the musicians, chorusing, "Beware!" or, "Woe!" at the right times.

The guests shed tears when Pluto dragged me off to the nether regions and my grieving mother searched the four corners of the earth for me. "Alas, the sky is gray," chorused the maids. "Alas, the fruit trees wither." The world was locked in barren winter, blighted by the goddess Demeter's sorrow.

Then the ladies wept again at the happy ending, when Persephone returns to the earth and her mother, bringing springtime. As the flute played a merry tune, I danced around our garden, scattering flowers. "Joy!" chorused the maids. "Joy," muttered Gundi, lifting the heavy Pluto mask from her head.

"How light-footed Salome was!" said the ladies afterward. My mother was pleased with herself and with me, and I felt a deep glow.

Now, the day before the full moon, Herodias invited her friends again for a new performance. This time we would act out the myth of Europa, a beautiful princess kidnapped by the god Zeus. Zeus transformed himself into a bull in a meadow at the edge of the sea, where Europa was playing. The princess was so charmed by this handsome, gentle animal that she climbed up on his back. At once he trotted into the waves with her—and the hapless maiden was never seen again.

As we practiced, Herodias noticed that Gundi and I, playing the two halves of the bull, were the weak part of this performance. My mother recited her lines with great feeling as she acted out the part of Europa. Two slaves rippled long, blue-green scarves along the ground in a good imitation of waves. But Gundi and I had a terrible time learning to move together as one animal inside our hide and horns. Especially with Herodias perched on the back.

"Alas!" cried Herodias, clinging to the hide.

Inside the bull, Gundi muttered, "I didn't mind so much playing the lord of the underworld. But the rear end of a bull—!"

On the afternoon of the performance, Gundi and I managed all right. Herodias sat gracefully on the back of the "bull," real-looking fear and sorrow on her expressive face. (I couldn't see, of course, but the guests complimented her on this afterward.) She spoke the last lines, the chorus of servants exclaimed, "Alas!" and the ladies applauded. As Herodias slipped from the hide, Gundi sighed with relief. "Oh, my aching bones."

"Dear friends," I heard my mother say to the guests in a still sorrowful voice, "Europa's story is not only a myth. Before long, I will indeed be borne across the sea by a mighty one."

What? What was she talking about? I squirmed to find a gap in the hide and peer out.

Herodias paused, posing with her left hand to her heart. I noticed a new gold ring, set with a large emerald, on her third finger. "I am leaving Herod Junior and marrying Herod Antipas. In a few days I will be the wife of the Tetrarch of Galilee and Perea." To a question from one of her friends she answered, "Yes, Salome will come with me."

Through the gap in the hide I cried out, "No!" My mother laughed a musical laugh, signaling not to take me seriously. The ladies laughed, too, maybe thinking that was a planned comic ending. I felt ashamed and confused. Gundi and I scuttled through the colonnade and shrugged off the hide. Gundi muttered, "I could have told you."

"Then why didn't you tell me?" I demanded. Before I even knew how angry I was, I slapped her face. Gundi staggered against a column. I hated myself, and I wanted to run away. At the same time, I didn't want to let anyone, especially my mother, know how upset I was.

Now that the play was over, the servants were bringing in refreshments, and the garden filled with chatter. I sat down glumly in a corner, leaning against the mosaic of the dancing maenad. The palm of my hand still stung from slapping Gundi.

One of the guests, the mother of a girl in my class at the Temple, spoke to me kindly. "Just think, Salome," she said. "In Galilee, you'll be a princess."

"Not really a princess, any more than Herodias will be a queen," I said. "Uncle Antipas is only a tetrarch, the ruler of a *quarter* of a kingdom."

The woman looked shocked at my rudeness, but she couldn't have been more shocked than I was to hear my own rude words. My mother heard me, too, and ordered me to my room.

That evening just before dinner, a messenger delivered a letter to Herodias from my father. He wrote from the house of Secundus, a Forum crony of his. She read the waxed tablet with her lip curled. "News travels quickly in Rome. I wonder which of my dear friends—or perhaps it was more than one?—informed Junior?" She handed the tablet to me. "Read; this is how much your father values his daughter."

It had crossed my mind that my father might want to keep me with him in Rome, and it would be his right to do so. But his letter ordered Herodias to remove herself and her belongings, "including the girl Salome," from his house. He'd already divorced Herodias, and he allowed her exactly one day, beginning at sunrise tomorrow, to accomplish the move.

Junior went on sarcastically, *I thank my former wife for her decision. Now I'll never have to put up with her good-for-nothing*

*brother Agrippa again. And I'm free to marry a younger woman*
*who will bear me sons. By the way, don't expect to get your dowry*
*back. I've already spent it.*

Although I didn't want to stay with my father, still, his
words were a slap in the face to me as well as Herodias. During the meal I picked at the food while my mother talked on
and on. Some of the time she spoke to me, and some of the
time she addressed her remarks to the wall beside us, to a
portrait of my father.

"Keep my dowry, then! Do you think I'll miss it? Antipas's coffers are overflowing with gold, and he denies me
nothing!" She flashed her emerald ring at the portrait. "Or
perhaps you think I mind leaving your house." She gave a
scornful laugh and turned to me. "The house Antipas keeps
in Rome is twice this size and in a better neighborhood. Wait
till you see it!"

I said nothing, but Herodias talked on, justifying herself.

"What you have to understand is that I was only thirteen
when they married me off to my uncle Junior. I had no choice
in the matter." Yes, I knew that her grandfather, King Herod
the Great of Judea, had commanded the marriage.

I also knew that my great-grandfather the king was not a
man to argue with. Gundi used to tell me some terrifying stories about him, always ending with something like, "And if

you don't stay in bed and go right to sleep, King Herod will grab you and lock you up in his dungeon."

I finally grew old enough to realize that the king of Judea, even if he were still alive, would probably not travel across the Mediterranean Sea to punish a naughty little girl. But from what everyone said, he was quick to torture or kill anyone who crossed him. Before he betrothed Herodias to Junior, he'd killed Aristobulus, Herodias's father. He'd also killed her grandmother Mariamne (his favorite wife!) and another of his sons, Alexander.

But King Herod had a sentimental streak, it seemed. He decided he'd been tricked into killing his son Aristobulus, and he was so sorry that he cried. He decided to make up for his mistake by arranging a fine marriage for his orphaned granddaughter Herodias. So my mother, a girl younger than I was now, became the bride of one of her father's half brothers, Herod Junior of Rome. Everyone agreed this match was a great honor for Herodias, because at that time, Junior was second in line to succeed his father as king of Greater Judea. With a little luck, the first heir, Antipater, would not live too long, and Junior would become King Herod II.

Tonight, listening to Herodias although I pretended not to, I gathered a new idea about why she'd been discontent with my father. Since I was a young child, it had seemed obvious to me that my mother had a right to be unhappy with her marriage. When my father was home, which wasn't often, he was cold and critical. And he was so much older than his niece-wife.

But now I understood her real complaint. It wasn't only my father who'd been deeply disappointed when old King Herod had changed his mind about the succession. As Herod Junior's wife, Herodias had expected to become queen of Greater Judea.

Before his death, Herod had accused Antipater of plotting against him and had him executed. He didn't execute my father, but he left him out of his final will entirely. Instead, Herod gave the best half of his kingdom, Judea and Samaria, to another son, Archelaus. The other half was divided between Antipas and Philip. Antipas received a quarter of the original kingdom, Galilee and Perea, while Philip received the poorest section, Gaulanitis.

None of the brothers was completely happy with this arrangement, but obviously Junior had the most to be unhappy about. He complained to his friends at the court of the Emperor Augustus, who had the final authority to confirm or discard the will of a client king. But it turned out that Archelaus, Antipas, and Philip had more powerful friends at court. So Herodias's husband would not become ruler of Greater Judea or of anything else except the estates in eastern Anatolia that he already owned. And Herodias would not become queen.

"If *I* had been old Herod's son," said Herodias, "I would have spent more time at my father's court in Judea and less time at the chariot races."

As the slaves cleared the platters from the dinner table, the doorkeeper appeared. Someone was outside: a litter from the Temple of Diana, an escort for Miss Salome.

# FOUR

# CALLED BY THE GODDESS?

I was so surprised that I said my first words of the evening, "For me?"

"Oh!—it's the full moon," said Herodias. "I forgot; I told the priestess that you could sleep at the Temple overnight to see if the goddess would give a sign. Well, I suppose you might as well go."

"I don't want to," I said. At that moment, I would have argued about anything Herodias told me to do.

"There's no point in offending the Temple, Salome." My mother spoke sharply, but then she went on in a persuasive tone, "It's only one night, sweet girl. Just make sure that in the morning, you tell the priestess that the goddess gave *no*

sign. Don't tell her any dream of yours, even something tri-
fling like eating honey cakes. The priestess of Diana is clever,
and you don't want to give her an excuse to say you have a
calling. She'd be delighted to have a Herod in the cult."

So I went with the escort, sullenly. A short while later,
I spread my pallet out in the darkened sanctuary of the
Temple. I didn't fall asleep right away, though. There was a
knot of anger in my chest. I was angry at Antipas for taking
my mother, and I was angry at my father for treating me as an
unwanted child.

But most of all, I was angry at my mother. She was the
one who'd truly betrayed me. She'd tricked me into believing
that we were best friends. What she really cared about was
being a queen, or at least living like one.

A few days ago, I remembered, Antipas had taken her to
the seagoing port of Puteoli to inspect the ship that would
carry him to Judea. "Antipas is having the *Ceres* completely
refitted!" she'd reported to me. "It'll be a floating palace." I'd
wondered why she was so enthusiastic about the ship, and
now I knew: it would be *her* floating palace. Queen Herodias.

Lying alone in the Temple, I missed the soothing sound
of Gundi's breathing. She'd slept in the same room with me
since I was a baby. I turned on my back and gazed up at the
great statue of Diana. The moon, sacred to the goddess,

shone through the columns of the portico and into the sanctuary. Diana, dressed in a short tunic, was striding forward. With one hand she reached toward the quiver on her back for an arrow, while the other hand held her bow in a relaxed grip. The hint of a smile softened her noble face.

Such a powerful, free being, this goddess. Suppose she did want me to serve her? A daring thought came to me, just the opposite of what my mother had instructed. If I wanted to serve Diana and stay in Rome, I could. I could say in the morning that the goddess had summoned me. Who would know?

Somehow this thought led to a new view of Herodias, as if I were standing on top of the roof and looking down at a small figure. Until now, she'd filled up the foreground of my life so that I couldn't see her whole. I'd been like a little child who sees only her nurse's skirt and feet.

It was a shock, like jumping from the steam room at the baths into the cold pool. Wildly mixed feelings swirled around in my head. I was thrilled with my new sense of power. But I also felt sad and anxious; shouldn't I protect that small Herodias, who didn't even know how weak she was?

Later I fell asleep, dreaming that I knelt before the statue of Diana. My chest hurt with a terrible longing. *Help me,* I begged her.

Gazing at me tenderly, Diana dropped her hand from the quiver and reached out. I took her hand, which was not stone cold, but warm and strong. I climbed up beside her—and we strode forward together.

In the morning I remembered the dream. The goddess had favored me, Salome! For a moment I lay basking in the memory.

Then my daring thought of last night returned, only now it seemed like something I could really choose to do. I felt dizzy with excitement.

Maybe it didn't matter that Herodias had gone off on her own path. *My* path opened up before me, and it didn't depend on Herodias. I was frightened but delighted, as if I were standing on the roof of the Temple—and realized that I had wings.

I told my dream to the priestess, stammering as I saw how deeply she was moved. Her eyes shone wetly. "Salome, my dear," she said, "you have the true calling. You will follow me as priestess of this Temple. We will make the arrangements with your family."

So I had done it. I would not go to Judea with Herodias and Antipas as they planned. Yes, *I* had chosen the shape of my life. Why was I terrified? This was what I wanted: to

move into the Temple compound, to devote myself to dancing and performing the sacred rites. At the next feast day of
Diana, I would make the vows of a priestess.

How could I be fearful when the goddess was leading
me? Guiltily I remembered Gundi and my promise to her,
but the priestess reassured me: I could bring a personal slave
with me to the Temple. Entering the service of Diana was
like entering into a marriage, and my family would furnish a
dowry.

And so I thought it was settled, and my fears faded. At
home, I found Herodias supervising the slaves as they packed
trunks. She hardly listened to my breathless announcement.
But then, taking in what I'd said, she turned on me.

"What is the matter with you?" Herodias shook me by
the shoulders. "I thought I made it plain that I was sending
you to the Temple only to go through the motions. Why did
you tell the priestess that dream? Why didn't you at least talk
to me first?"

"It—it was a dream from the goddess," I stammered. I
knew my mother wasn't pious—either about the Greek and
Roman gods or about the Jewish faith—but I was shocked
that my dream seemed to mean nothing to her. "Diana chose
me for her own."

Herodias made a scornful noise. "The priestess put the

idea for that dream into your head, you silly girl. Didn't I warn you? And what an old-fashioned idea." She laughed, a musical sound. "No one really believes in Diana anymore."

For a moment I doubted myself, but then I felt angry that Herodias wouldn't honor my dream. *My* dream, not a dream that the priestess had slipped into my head. "The goddess has called me," I said in a loud voice, "and I must join the Temple."

"Salome." Calming herself, Herodias pulled me down beside her on a chest. "You don't understand what you want to throw away. Perhaps for another girl in your class, it would be an honor to take the vows at the Temple. But you are something more, much more, than a Roman girl of good family. You are a Herod, of the ruling family of the Jews."

I wouldn't look at her. "Diana herself called me to walk with her," I said.

"In fact, you are of royal blood, of a line of Jewish rulers even older than the Herods. Through your great-grandmother Mariamne, you are descended from Queen Salome Alexandra of the proud Hasmonean dynasty."

Of royal blood . . . Perhaps if my mother had spoken these words before Uncle Antipas came to Rome, I would have been thrilled. But now I was sure she was bringing up my royal blood only to get me to go along quietly. Twisting a strand of my hair, I stared blankly at the pile of colored silks on the couch.

"Stop that!" Herodias slapped at my fingers. "Are you listening to me?"

"Yes, *Herodias*," I said.

Giving a deep sigh, Herodias changed her tack. "Don't talk about leaving me." She sounded as if her heart would break. "Salome, you're my dearest friend. How could I possibly travel to the ends of the earth without you?" She laid her hand on the side of my face. "My sweet girl! Men are a necessary evil, but my own . . ."

Herodias, for all her beauty and charm, needed me more than anyone else! I melted like a lump of butter in the sun. Herodias picked up my hand, and it seemed that she was displacing Diana's hand. Last night's dream, so real at the moment I awoke, turned pale and thin. And I was relieved, to tell the truth.

On the way to the baths that afternoon, I told Gundi about my dream of Diana and my plan to take my old nurse to the Temple with me. I thought Gundi would be grateful that I'd remembered her wish. But my main point was how much my mother loved me, so much that she'd struggled with the goddess for me.

Gundi, however, had a different view. "I could have told

you they wouldn't let you do that." She sniffed. "I heard them talking, before she announced the divorce." By "them" Gundi meant my mother and Antipas. They'd been discussing how my father would react to his wife's leaving him for his half brother.

According to Gundi, Antipas had asked my mother, "Will Junior let her go?" (Gundi imitated the Tetrarch's deep, smooth voice, with her northern barbarian accent on top of it—it would have been funny, except for what she was saying.) "Sometimes," Antipas told Herodias, "I don't believe he thinks of anything but the chariot races. But he must know that a bride's worth many times the value of her dowry as a bond in a political alliance."

"No, he's hopeless," Herodias had said. "It's better that we don't say anything about Salome. It would be just like Junior to insist on keeping her for spite."

It made me sick to imagine my mother talking about me that way to her lover. "Shut your mouth, barbarian drudge." I almost slapped her again, but then I remembered how bad I'd felt the last time.

Later, floating in the warm pool, I told myself that Gundi was making it up. I was no longer a little child, to be frightened by her stories about the evil Herods.

\* \* \*

At the wedding, Herodias was radiant in the blond wig she wore on special occasions. There were many important guests to see how the fair hair set off her wide dark eyes. The marriage of Herodias to Antipas was a big social event in Rome, with Roman nobles and foreign dignitaries as well as Antipas's own courtiers among the guests.

At the wedding banquet, I was seated at a table for older children. I didn't know any of them, and I wasn't in a mood to make friends. Anyway, we were leaving for Judea in a few days. I slumped on my dining couch, fingering the gold bracelet that the happy couple had given me. Its shape, a snake with two heads and no tail, was supposed to mean long life. To me, it looked more like an image of my mother and stepfather.

# FIVE

# HOW SHALL I LIVE?

The first day of the voyage, leaning over the side to watch the coastline slide by, I unthinkingly twisted the gold bracelet on my wrist. This bracelet Antipas and Herodias had given me was finely wrought, the most costly piece of jewelry I'd ever owned. I shouldn't have been wearing it on an ordinary day, I suppose.

I swear I didn't know the bracelet was falling off until the instant it slid over my knuckles. Before I could even grab for it, it flashed through the air and disappeared, hidden by the glare on the water. At first I was horrified. Herodias and Antipas would be so angry.

Then I thought, *I'm* the one who's angry. I'm stuck on

this ship so I can't even get away from being ignored. I have to sit here and watch Herodias and her Bull, like watching a very boring and annoying play called *The Happy Couple*. Why can't Herodias think about me for a change instead of gazing into that man's eyes as if only the two of them were on board?

I was angrier than I'd realized. I thought, Let the bracelet be a sacrifice to Poseidon, god of the sea. Maybe he'll send a storm to wreck our ship.

No—no—no! "Lord of the sea"—I hastily made a substitute petition—"accept my offering and bring our ship safely to Caesarea."

By the second day, I felt so restless I almost wished for a shipwreck again. "If only I could go to the baths and swim," I complained to Gundi. "If only I could be at the Temple of Diana for a few hours, dancing . . . If only I could have stayed at the Temple forever!"

"Past is past," said Gundi briskly. "Forget about Diana. Aphrodite will be your protector now." Every night Gundi said charms over me, and she claimed that Antipas's courtiers could hardly take their eyes off me. With meaningful glances at my newly curved body, she reminded me that Aphrodite was supposed to have been born from the sea.

I'd noticed the men stealing glances at me, but I thought

they were probably wondering how I could be so awkward. My body was indeed changing, but the main result seemed to be that I was even clumsier. Being at sea didn't help, either. The ship plunged down into the troughs of the waves and up over the crests; it wallowed from side to side; it rocked back and forth.

I suppose Herodias did think of me a little, because she came up with an idea to keep me occupied during the voyage. On the third day aboard the *Ceres,* she proposed that Leander should give me lessons to improve my Greek. "My secretary?" said Antipas with a frown at me. "Leander is a highly educated philosophy scholar. I can hardly order him to work as a peda-gogue, tutoring a young girl."

Herodias glanced at him from under her eyelashes. "Oh," she said. "My prince, I beg your pardon. I thought you could order anyone to do . . . anything you wanted." She gave one of her mischievous giggles. "But not with our Socrates, I guess."

Herodias had her way. Beginning on the bright, brisk April day that we left Syracuse, Leander met with me every fair afternoon. Gundi, of course, sat in on my lessons as chaperone.

I was embarrassed at first that Leander was forced to tutor me. But he was patient and polite—I gathered that he

felt rather sorry for me. At the end of the first lesson, I asked
him to show me which direction Rome lay in. He explained
how to find northwest from the position of the sun or stars.

"And your city, Alexandria?" I asked. "What direction is
Alexandria?"

Leander smiled wistfully. "Ah, Alexandria. My city lies
southeast—exactly the opposite direction."

The *Ceres* wallowed through the waves day by day, and
each afternoon the three of us met in the shelter of the
striped mainsail. Gundi always brought wool and a spindle
to spin thread. She hummed a spinning song to herself, even
while Leander was declaiming poetry.

After a few days, Leander and I got into the habit of playing a game of checkers after the lesson. Gundi spun her
thread as always and gave advice (mostly bad) on moves. The
simple game didn't take much concentration, and we chatted
as we played. I found out about his father's last request: it
had to do with Leander's three sisters. They were depending
on him to send home money for their dowries.

If it weren't for his mother and sisters, Leander would
have stayed in Alexandria to continue his philosophy studies.
But after his father died suddenly last fall and his business
was sold to pay debts, it was up to Leander to provide for the

family. Just as he was wondering how to do that, the Tetrarch of Galilee had stopped in Alexandria on his way to Rome.

Leander had heard that Antipas was looking for a new secretary and that the Tetrarch of Galilee paid well—very well. So Leander had joined Antipas's court and come to Rome.

"It doesn't seem fitting for a philosopher to work as a secretary," I said.

Leander gave me a wry smile. "I thought there would be . . . compensations. I imagined that with Prince Antipas as my patron, I'd have the chance to visit some fine private libraries. I'd read rare books and talk with learned scholars."

Most of the times I'd seen him, Leander had been moping around our atrium while Antipas visited Herodias. "What does a secretary actually do?" I asked. "Do you write letters?"

Leander nodded. "Mainly letters, mainly to Chuza, the Tetrarch's steward in Galilee. Also, the Tetrarch has me take notes on all his business and political dealings." He shrugged. "I can't object; I knew I'd be doing that kind of work for Prince Antipas. It's only that I thought the company would be rather different."

I asked what he meant, "different." Leander looked

embarrassed as he explained. "You see, the Jews I know in Alexandria belong to the school of the philosopher Philo. Even though I don't share their faith, I respect their devotion to their Law. They are true seekers of the path of virtue, men with noble minds."

"So you expected Antipas and his court to be like Philo and his school?" I asked.

"I suppose I did." Leander's face reddened. "At least a little."

I felt sorry for him, making such a foolish mistake. Antipas, a man with a noble mind!

We were a week into the voyage before Leander told me what he hated most about serving the Tetrarch. It was taking dictation from Antipas while he composed his journal entries. "The Tetrarch fancies himself a philosopher-prince," said Leander with a pained expression. "That's why he hired me instead of an ordinary scribe—he wanted a secretary who understood Deep Thoughts."

"Antipas has Deep Thoughts?" I asked in amazement. "What are they like?"

"Drivel," groaned Leander.

Day followed day, sometimes so bright that my eyes ached from the glare, sometimes so stormy that everyone but the

sailors stayed in the cabins. At night I often lay awake, turning restlessly and making up stories for myself. My favorite
was a story that began, What if, through no fault of mine, our
ship was wrecked? And what if Leander and I were the only
survivors?

I shivered at my own daring. I had to keep reassuring myself that no one could know my private stories. I imagined
Leander and me lounging on the shore of our private island.
All alone with no chaperone, no mother or stepfather, no
rules about whom to marry. We'd recite Greek poetry to each
other, and our eyes would meet, and then our lips, and . . .

Somehow, even though it was my made-up story,
drowned bodies began washing up on the imaginary beach.
What a monster I was, to wish for a shipwreck! Gundi didn't
deserve to die, and neither did the crew. I didn't really want
even Herodias and Antipas to drown. Squirming into a fresh
position on my bed, I started the story over again without
killing anyone: What if the goddess Aphrodite magically
transported Leander and me to an undiscovered island?

The one thing I looked forward to on the *Ceres* was
my Greek lesson. I was always taken aback, though, that the
Leander who taught me Greek wasn't the Leander of my
dreams. He *looked* like the dream Leander, with curly hair
hanging over his forehead and deep-set hazel eyes. But the

real Leander, instead of murmuring in my ear, kept correcting my pronunciation.

The day before we stopped at Crete for fresh water, Herodias finally seemed to remember me. She came up to me that overcast morning as I stood at the ship's railing. I was still angry but almost ready to make up, if Herodias seemed really sorry.

"The captain says the sea can be rough in April," remarked Herodias, "but so far the sailing hasn't been bad."

I gazed steadily in the direction of Rome. The gray-green sea stretched in every direction, but I could tell northwest by the position of the sun, only half hidden by clouds.

"And dolphins are following the ship," continued Herodias. "That's supposed to be lucky."

"I'd feel *lucky*," I said, "if we were on our way to Rome and the Temple of Diana." Didn't she realize that she owed me an apology? The wind blew a strand of hair across my face, and I caught it and twined it in my fingers.

Herodias made an impatient noise. "If you're so devoted to the goddess, you can worship her just as well in Tiberias as in Rome. I'm sure they have shrines to Diana in Tiberias. Or if they don't, Antipas will build one."

"What good will that do me?" I asked, still staring across

the sea. "I won't be staying in Tiberias for long." In a sharper voice I added, "I'll be married off as the glue in some political alliance."

"Oh, Salome. My own child." I was startled by the heartfelt tone in Herodias's voice. "My little one, this is our fate. You have to understand that a woman *must* marry, and a woman of a royal family *must* marry to advance the fortunes of the dynasty."

I felt a brief surge of pity for the child-bride Herodias, married off to my cold, neglectful father. Then my anger at her returned, and I answered, "Oh, I thought that some women—at least, one—married to advance their own fortunes."

Pulling back from me, Herodias laughed the light, musical laugh that she used for ridicule. "My, what a sulk we're in. No one's making you marry right this minute. Meanwhile, you can still enjoy your daydreams about the handsome Greek secretary. But try to be more discreet."

My face burned with shame. How could she know my secret thoughts about Leander? How dare she mention them?

"But my dear chick," she went on, "I would never consent to betroth you to anyone distasteful. I pledge before Diana, my precious daughter will not suffer the same fate that I did."

That was the last straw, swearing by Diana. "What a mighty pledge!" I said. "Only the other day, you told me no one believed in Diana anymore."

I waited for her to deny it, but Herodias merely shrugged and walked away.

Shortly after we left Crete, something happened to take my mind off my own fate. Simon, the youngest of the Tetrarch's courtiers, disappeared.

I found out about this early on a foggy morning, when Antipas called the passengers together at the stern of the ship. According to the guards, he explained, Simon had stayed up late the night before, drinking wine and throwing dice with the captain of the guards. Afterward, he must have stumbled on his way to bed and fallen overboard, unnoticed by the sailors on watch.

That's strange, I thought. It didn't seem like Simon to drink and gamble with the captain of the guards. That wasn't the way to advance his career. I glanced around the group to see if any of the others seemed surprised.

The expressions of Antipas's courtiers and their servants were as blank as the scene around the ship. The fog this morning was so thick and chill and the sea so calm that the *Ceres* hardly appeared to move. The ship seemed to float on the fog, rather than on the water. I wondered if it was like this on the river Styx, the stream that separated the land of the living from the land of the dead.

Antipas gave a long, flowery speech about what a talented, delightful young man Simon had been, with a bright future ahead of him. Antipas would never forgive himself, he said, for his untimely death. Then Antipas pronounced the prayers for the departed. He dropped into the sea two silver denarii, the coins that ordinarily would have been placed on Simon's eyes so he could pay for the ferry over the Styx. Then Antipas said, "I must retire to grieve and compose a letter of condolence to Simon's mother."

That afternoon Leander was very quiet, and he seemed to have a hard time paying attention to the lesson. When I recited an ode for him, he didn't even notice that I'd finished at first. Then he pulled his gaze back from the horizon and said absently, "Well done, Miss Salome. You had the accent and the feeling there."

"It's a beautiful poem," I said, puzzled by his praise. I might have had the feeling, but I knew my accent still wasn't right.

"Yes, the words are beautiful." He paused, then burst out, "Beauty isn't enough, is it? What about justice?"

On a hunch, I asked the question on my mind. "Do you know what happened to Simon?"

Leander looked alarmed. He glanced around to see if anyone was listening, but the only one within earshot was Gundi. My chaperone sat dozing on a coil of rope with her mouth open, her scarf pulled forward to shade her eyes.

In a low voice Leander answered, "The servants are whispering that Simon found too much favor with Sejanus, the Emperor's regent. That Simon was talked about as a rival for the throne of Galilee and Perea."

Foolish Simon? Who would imagine that he could rule an apartment block, let alone a tetrarchy? My face must have showed my surprise, because Leander said, "Exactly—Simon didn't have the wits to rule a henhouse. But he wouldn't be the first ruler without any qualifications. Maybe Sejanus thought he'd be easier to control than Antipas."

I thought of something else. "But Simon is—was—the Tetrarch's nephew. At least, his half sister's son."

"Yes," said Leander in a flat tone. "I suppose Simon—and his mother, who sent him on this trip—thought his kinship would keep him safe."

The air was clear this afternoon, but I still felt in a fog. "Maybe the servants are wrong about what happened."

Leander started to speak, then stopped and shook his head.

One afternoon several days later, Leander remarked,

"They say we'll sight the coast of Judea tomorrow or perhaps the next day."

So the voyage was almost over, and soon these lessons would be ended. I studied Leander's expression to see if he seemed sorry. But he launched briskly into a comparison of different poetic styles.

After the lesson, though, while we were playing checkers, he said in a low tone, "Do you ever wonder about the question, How shall I live?" I was surprised, and before I could answer, he laughed nervously. "Forgive me; that was an idle question. Girls don't study philosophy."

I felt a little insulted. "I could wonder, but what good would it do me?" I snapped. "I can't choose how to live. They'll make me marry some disgusting old goat." I dropped my gaze to the checkerboard.

"Miss Salome," said Gundi without taking her eyes off her spindle, "I don't think this is a proper conversation for a young lady to have with her step-father's secretary."

"I agree," said Leander in an odd tone of voice, "so let's not speak of ourselves or anyone we know. Let's consider an imaginary problem in ethics: A certain man serves an evil master. But he works for a good reason, to pay his sisters' dowries. That is his duty to his family and his vow to his dying father."

I listened without commenting, although it was easy enough to guess who the man was, as well as his evil master.

"The master, though evil, pays very well," continued Leander. "If the man left this master, he couldn't get another such position, and his sisters might be past childbearing age before he could get them married off properly. What should he do? Surely it is wrong to serve the evil master. But it would be wrong also not to follow his father's deathbed request."

"Why, that's clear as water," said Gundi with a sniff. "Family duty comes first, so the fellow should serve his master until he's paid his sisters' dowries. Then he can cut the evil master's throat, which he deserves, and escape in the middle of the night."

Leander gave her an outraged look, but I couldn't hold back a snort of laughter. Then I said soberly, "Only the mighty ones can truly do as they wish. That's why I wanted to serve Diana, because—" My voice caught on the last words. I remembered my dream, when I took the goddess's hand, and my feeling of striding forward toward adventure.

Leander shook his head, leaning forward earnestly. "But might doesn't get us justice. Think of the stories about the gods and the heroes. Yes, they're powerful, but they're ruled by their passions. For example, Zeus falls in love with

Europa, so he turns himself into a bull and kidnaps her. He never stops to consider, Is my course of action right? Is it just? He feels a passion, and he acts on it."

"The gods don't have to ask themselves what is right or what is just!" Gundi put in. "They are—the gods, that's all."

"Yes, they can do whatever they wish." Leander looked directly at me, although he was answering Gundi. "But is that admirable? There must be a higher standard than that, or life would be senseless." He glanced over his shoulder as if he felt danger. But he went on, "I do not admire power unless it is used in a good way."

Staring at him, I drew in a long breath and let it out. Leander's words were deeply satisfying to me. For a moment we were silent, and even Gundi only made a disapproving *tsk, tsk.* The sound of the pennants snapping at the top of the mast seemed loud. Then Leander looked down at the checkerboard. "It's your move, Miss Salome."

That was all there was to it, but that night I lay awake, whispering to myself, "It's your move," and remembering the look in his beautiful eyes. He knew I'd understood what he was hinting about. What if I told Herodias and she told Antipas? If the Tetrarch could do away with his half nephew Simon, why would he hesitate to kill a Greek secretary?

For some reason, though, Leander felt he could trust me. It was as if he'd opened a window and shown me a new world—a world of goodness and truth. That glimpse seemed more precious than the gold bracelet I'd dropped to the bottom of the sea, and I hugged it to my heart.

# SIX

# A WARNING

The sun had set across the Jordan River, and John and his disciples sat outside a cave in the bluffs. Over the crackling of their fire, they heard a pebble rattle on the nearby path. A deer, perhaps, or a jackal? Just in case, the disciples picked up sticks of firewood.

John, weary to the bone, did not move. All morning long he had preached while throngs gathered to listen. All afternoon he had baptized people. Now he was so tired that he shivered, although it wasn't really cold. Here in the Jordan Valley, the nights were never suddenly sharp, as they were out in the wilderness.

Elias, John's closest disciple, had been watching him with concern. As he tossed another stick on the fire, the flames flared up. "Who goes there?" exclaimed Elias. The other disciples jumped to their feet.

The widened circle of firelight revealed a single man—a soldier, studs glinting on his leather kilt. Elias and another disciple moved between the stranger and their leader.

Holding up his empty hands, the soldier took a step closer to the fire. "Peace, Rabbi," he said to John.

"Peace to you," said John. He noted the man's blue cape, the uniform of Herod Antipas's troops. He waited for the soldier to explain why he had come alone to see the Baptizer.

"Rabbi," said the stranger, "take my advice: leave for the wilderness while you still can. In a few days the Tetrarch will return from Rome and hear what you say about his new marriage. My officer is only waiting for his order to arrest you. It's not safe for you in this place."

"No," retorted Elias, "not if *you* lead his enemies here."

The soldier glanced at Elias, but he spoke again to John. "Rabbi, they all know where you sleep. The Romans know, and so does the High Priest, as well as us from the Tetrarch's fortress." He gestured in the direction of Macherus. "You should leave this place."

John nodded, but he didn't move. He would have been glad to go back to the wilderness, to the wide lonely spaces and the dry sounds of wind in brush and rocks. But the Lord had called him to the Jordan River, and here he would stay as long as the Lord willed it.

The soldier sighed. He turned as if to go, then turned back. In a low, shy voice he asked, "How could a soldier— what could I do to show repentance, Rabbi?"

As tired as he was, John stood up at once and put his hands on the man's shoulders. He looked into his eyes. "Don't use your uniform and sword to rob the people," he said. "Antipas pays you, doesn't he?" The man nodded. "Then live on your wages."

One of the disciples made a skeptical snort, and John knew what he was thinking. A *soldier* not bully and rob the people? It was unheard of. But this soldier nodded again, so John went on, "When you've lived this way for a month, come back, and I'll baptize you."

"Thank you, Rabbi." The soldier's voice trembled. "Rabbi! Please go, before it's too late." When John didn't answer, he threw up his hands. "Heaven be my witness, I warned him!" Turning again, he disappeared into the shadows.

# SEVEN

# CAESAREA

"Antipas should reign in that city, his own father's city," said Herodias. "It's only right. When the Emperor deposed Archelaus as ruler of Judea, why didn't he install Antipas in his place? There was no need to bring in a Roman governor."

We were on deck, gazing toward Caesarea Maritima. This was the end of our voyage, the port city of Judea.

As the city seemed to grow behind its lighthouse, Herodias pointed out its features to me: the splendid harbor, the Temple of Roma and Augustus Caesar, the theater facing the sea. "All built by Herod the Great."

My stepfather joined us at the railing just as Herodias

was saying, "And the big marble building on the point, north of the harbor—"

"—is the Governor's palace," Antipas interrupted her. He added dryly, "Or I should say, the palace of my father, Herod the Great."

Herodias gave him a sly glance from under her eyelashes. "And perhaps one day, the palace of the new king of the Jews."

I was alarmed by the reckless way she was talking, but a smile creased the corners of Antipas's eyes. "For the time being," he drawled, "we'll allow Governor Pilate to lodge there."

I felt queasy. What did they mean? Did they think Antipas could grow mighty enough to force the Roman Empire out of Judea? Between their treason-ous hints and the choppy water outside the harbor, my stomach bobbed dangerously. I felt chilled in spite of the mild day, and I kept my arms wrapped inside my woolen cloak. Even after the ship swept under the stone lighthouse and into calm water, I still felt cold and shaken.

On the broad walkway above the docks, a group of guards and courtiers waited for the Tetrarch and his party. An earnest-looking man, balding but not old, greeted Antipas

with a low bow. "Thanks be to the gods for your safe arrival, my prince."

Antipas presented the man to Herodias and me as his steward, Chuza. My mother, putting on a queenly air, inquired graciously about his wife's health.

"It is good of my lady to ask," answered the steward. "Joanna is afflicted with a weakness in her limbs. She does go to the hot springs—my lord kindly lets her use the royal bathhouse—and the waters give her some relief."

As our group proceeded up the walkway to the temple, Steward Chuza briefed the Tetrarch on the plans for our stay in Caesarea. "The Governor gives a banquet in your honor tonight, my lord. Then five days of games, beginning tomorrow. But I explained that you had pressing business in Galilee and couldn't stay here any longer than two days."

Antipas nodded. "Good, good. Pilate will enjoy his games more without me, and so will I. What else?"

Chuza went on with his report. There had been a recent letter from Antipas's half brother Philip, Tetrarch of Gaulanitis, accepting Antipas's invitation to his birthday feast. Chuza looked sideways at me as he said this, and my stepfather and Herodias exchanged glances. I was afraid I knew what that was about—using me as the glue in a family alliance.

Chuza brought up the business affairs of the tetrarchy

town by town. In Capernaum, he reported, the elders of the Jewish assembly wanted money to repair their west wall, damaged by a recent earthquake. Antipas grumbled, "I've poured enough money into that assembly hall already, for very little gratitude. All right—as long as they carve my name into a stone in the wall. My name at eye level, not down where only the dogs could read it."

In Magdala, Chuza went on, the tax collector was having trouble on his rounds. "Boys throwing rotten onions, sometimes stones." Antipas agreed to send two extra soldiers to Magdala as long as the tax collector paid a surcharge for the protection. "What about the unrest in the south?"

"It's been made worse by Governor Pilate's blunders in Jerusalem."

"More blunders?" asked Antipas. He explained to Herodias, "On Pilate's first trip to Jerusalem—didn't anyone tell him it's our holy city?—he marched his troops through the gates holding up the regimental standards. The standards, with the Emperor's image—blasphemy!" Antipas chuckled. "The Governor nearly had a bloodbath on his hands."

Chuza told him the latest: the Governor had built a new aqueduct for the city, thinking the people of Jerusalem would be grateful. But since he'd used money from the Jewish Temple, they called it sacrilege. Antipas rolled his eyes.

"As for the unrest in your own realm, I believe I mentioned the Baptizer in my last letter," Chuza continued as we climbed the wide steps to the temple. "The one who calls sinners to repent, who announces the coming of a mighty one? Recently the preacher was bold enough to criticize you by name. I didn't take any action, sir, since I expected you back soon."

Antipas nodded. "Good, good."

The group stopped in front of the huge painted statues of the late Emperor Augustus and of Roma, goddess of the city of Rome. A slave held out a basin and towel for Antipas, and he washed and dried his hands. "Yes, you did well," the Tetrarch went on to Chuza. "That John Baptizer bears watching, but I don't want to draw more attention to him."

The court all stood waiting for the Tetrarch to pour out libations of wine in front of the statues of Augustus and Roma and to say the ritual words of thanksgiving for a safe voyage. Antipas squinted up at the statue of the Emperor, lost in thought. "And who knows what's meant by 'the Mighty One'?" he mused. "It could be the Baptizer himself doesn't understand his prophecy."

Maybe Herodias finally realized how deeply she'd hurt me and was trying to make up by treating me like an adult. It seemed I was included in the formal dinner tonight. This would be my first real dinner party, not counting the horrible wedding banquet. Also, Herodias had told Gundi she could choose one of her fine *stolae* for me to wear tonight.

When I returned from the baths to my guest room, Gundi showed me the *stola* she'd picked. I gasped. It was one of Herodias's best, a butter yellow silk with gold thread embroidery in the border. The cloth had been imported, at great expense, from a land far beyond the Euphrates River. "Did Herodias say I could wear that?"

Ignoring my question, Gundi draped the *stola* around the curves of my body and fastened it with a silk cord. There was a mischievous twinkle in her eyes, and she chanted a little song to Freya, a northern name for Aphrodite.

"Hush that silly song!" I told her, laughing breathlessly.

While I sat on a stool, Gundi pinned up my hair and crimped the locks around my face with a curling iron. She fastened a gold-and-pearl necklace around my throat and hung gold earrings set with opals from my ears.

"Gundi, what are you doing?" I protested. "This is the jewelry Herodias was married in."

"Yes, so suitable for a young girl," said Gundi blandly. "Iris told me that Lady Herodias wouldn't be wearing these tonight." She added gold bangles for my wrists.

I didn't have a mirror—Gundi must have decided it would be too much to sneak off with my mother's mirror, which she'd miss right away. But the parts of myself I could see, I didn't recognize. When I stood up, the jewelry gleamed on my arms and chest and the yellow silk slithered over my body, as rich and soft as butter.

Chuckling to herself, Gundi pushed me out the door through the colonnade joining the guest quarters to the palace. Antipas's courtiers were already waiting there; their eyes widened as they caught sight of me. Antipas and Herodias appeared, decked out in ornate robes and glittering with jewels.

When Herodias saw me, her eyebrows shot up almost to her blond wig. Stepping toward me, she pretended to adjust a lock of my hair. "I didn't say you could borrow the yellow silk," she hissed. "Or those earrings."

I shrugged, wide-eyed. "Oh, Gundi thought you did."

Meanwhile, Antipas stared like a bull noticing a new heifer in his herd. His look seemed to strike sparks off my bare arms.

I should have been nervous, but instead, the eyes on me gave me confidence. Holding my head high, I followed my mother and stepfather as they followed Antipas's bodyguards into the palace dining hall. Servants placed wreaths of flowers on our heads, and we took our places on couches at the Governor's table.

After this grand beginning, though, the evening was disappointing. At our table the servers had to wait while Antipas's taster tried each dish—that spoiled the festive effect a bit. Also, the conversation was strained since Governor Pilate seemed bent on offending my stepfather.

"I hear from my men in Jerusalem that a new preacher's stirring up the rabble of Perea," said the Roman governor. "My deputy keeps an eye on him when he crosses the Jordan River into Judea."

"Do you mean John, called the Baptizer?" Antipas answered Pilate. With the point of his knife he speared one of the olives stuffed with anchovies. "I've been aware of his activities for some time."

As if they were playing tug-of-war, the Governor came right back. "A pretty bold fellow, isn't he? Now if it were me, I wouldn't like to hear a desert preacher tell me who I could and could not marry."

Antipas suddenly changed his tack and gazed gratefully at Governor Pilate. "Why, this John *is* overly bold. I see that now." His voice throbbed with sincerity. "While other peoples cannot hope to equal Roman expertise in governing, we can profit much by observing your example."

Pilate frowned, and you could see him wondering if the Tetrarch was having a joke at his expense. Antipas, smiling humbly, touched his hand to his forehead in a gesture of deference.

At this moment I happened to be lifting to my mouth a leg of grilled quail in onion sauce. Remembering the talk earlier today about Governor Pilate's blunders in Jerusalem, I gave a nervous giggle. The Governor, his wife, and everyone else at the head table looked at me. Trying to cover up my giggle with a cough, I spattered onion sauce onto the front of the borrowed yellow silk.

Herodias rolled her eyes. She said laughingly to Procula, the Governor's wife, "I'd thought my daughter was old enough to attend your dinner, but it seems I misjudged. Look how she's spoiled the *stola* I let her borrow! And it isn't pleasant for you to watch such bad table manners. I apologize for her."

Procula murmured something polite, but I wanted to vanish. Just a short while ago, I'd been transformed into a woman. I'd seen my beauty in the eyes of everyone who looked at me. Now I was a clumsy, overgrown child again. Ducking my head, I wished I'd stayed back in my room with Gundi. Although wasn't Gundi to blame? She'd not only sneaked Herodias's clothes and jewelry for me, but filled my head with her nonsense about Aphrodite.

It seemed as if that embarrassing moment went on forever, but finally the servers cleared the platters of quail and offered fruit and pastries. Even better, dancers in bead-fringed costumes leaped into the hall, taking attention from me. As I relaxed a bit, I swayed to the music, remembering how sweet it was to be transported in the sacred dances at the Temple of Diana.

These entertainers were surefooted and graceful, and the swinging beads accented their movements. But they didn't look transported any more than the slaves who'd served the dinner. By their expressions, the dancers might as well have been passing platters of baked fish.

"Huh." To Herodias, Antipas made a scornful noise under his breath. "These are the same entertainers Pilate hired the last time I came through Caesarea. He could do better—if he knew what 'better' was."

"Few men have your discerning taste in the arts, my lord," said Herodias.

"Not Romans, anyway," agreed Antipas as a slave refilled his wine goblet. "They like to think they invented civilization when all they really invented is good roads and good toilets."

Herodias, trilling her musical laugh, pressed Antipas's arm. I glanced uneasily at the Roman Governor. Pilate, clapping in time to the music, seemed to have missed this jab, but his wife squinted at us suspiciously. Antipas and Herodias beamed back at her like grateful guests.

Later, back in my room, Gundi was eager to hear about the dinner. "Was Lady Herodias wearing my hair?"

"What nonsense are you talking?" Gundi's knot of sand-colored, gray-streaked hair had been on her own head all evening. And why would Herodias want to wear it, anyway?

"You didn't know?" asked Gundi. "That's why she bought me years ago—for my hair as yellow as beaten flax. She had it sheared off and made into a wig. Then, when she was expecting you, she kept me to be your nursemaid. Oh, yes, that blond wig is my hair."

I was amazed. Why didn't I know this? Of course, ever since I'd been old enough to notice the color of my nurse-maid's hair, it had been grayish. It was hard to imagine a young, really blond Gundi.

"For a year or more," Gundi went on as she unpinned my *stola*, "I was so ashamed, going about with cropped hair. But I made great sport for her ladyship." There was a harsh note in her voice. "Once, at the baths with her friends, she pulled off my head scarf and pretended to think I was a man. 'A man sneaked into the women's baths!' she shouted, and they all laughed."

I stared at Gundi, thinking of the grudge my nursemaid had hidden all these years. But quickly Gundi put on the false smile with which slaves cover up their feelings. "No matter," she said cheerily. Loosening the silk cord of my *stola*, she helped me undress. "Was Cupid busy for you this evening? Who did he pierce with his arrows of love?"

"Never mind Cupid—Herodias was not pleased with me!" I grabbed the *stola* before she could fold it up. "Look— *onion sauce.*" I added, "She made me take her jewelry off as soon as we were out of the dining hall."

Gundi smiled. "No, it wouldn't please that one to see how Freya-Aphrodite favors you. But come on, who was smitten by the sight of you?" She kept asking until I admitted that the courtiers had stared at me.

"And so did—" I stopped. It seemed better not to speak of my stepfather.

Gundi seemed satisfied. Humming to herself, she shook out a drop of scented oil before her statuette of Aphrodite. I recognized that blue-glass scent bottle—it, too, was my mother's.

# EIGHT

# BANDITS

The morning after Pilate's banquet, there were chariot races. Before we went to the stadium, Herodias came to my room with a present. "Dear Salome, I've been selfish. I think *you* should have these opal earrings. Don't protest—I know you want them! And they do look sweet on you. Suitable for a young girl."

As Herodias fastened the opal earrings in my ears, I couldn't help noticing the jewels bright as pomegranate seeds—but much larger—dangling from Herodias's earlobes. She saw my gaze and smiled. "Do you like my new earrings? Antipas surprised me with them this morning. These are rubies, set in platinum." She lowered her eyelashes demurely.

"He looked into my eyes and quoted that Jewish proverb, 'A good wife who can find? Her price is far above rubies.' I was so touched."

Herodias was flying high that morning. In the stadium, as the Tetrarch Herod Antipas and his wife were seated in the Governor's pavilion, there was a flourish of trumpets. I caught a glimpse of her radiant face.

The rest of Antipas's court took their seats behind the couple, and everyone hurried to make bets. Antipas favored the Orange team, so of course Herodias, Chuza, and the Tetrarch's courtiers wore orange ribbons and bet on Orange. Governor Pilate and his officials were backers of the Greens.

I was caught up in the excitement, but just to be different, I decided to put my money on White. "Leander," I said as he climbed the stadium steps past my seat, "a denarius that White wins the first race!"

Leander bowed to me, but he shook his head. "On principle, I don't gamble, Miss Salome. Gambling gives honor to blind Luck."

"It's just for fun," I protested. Leander could be such a stick.

With a glum smile he admitted, "In any case, I don't have any money. I just sent my wages to my mother."

Of course, Leander's money was promised to his sisters'

dowry fund. I was a little ashamed of forgetting that, especially when I heard Antipas's bodyguards teasing the secretary. "Gambling gives honor to blind Luck," one man told
the others in a mincing voice.

The guards guffawed, and another man called out, "The
Greek would rather be back at the palace, reading a *scroll*!" I
glanced over my shoulder at Leander, who certainly did look
as if he wanted to be in a garden with Plato, not in the stadium among loud, sweaty soldiers. Today the guards were
worked up into a feverish excitement.

I sat with Gundi right behind Antipas and Herodias. As
the chariots lined up for the first race, Antipas was busy laying a wager with Governor Pilate. On the track below, a gong
sounded, and the horses sprang forward. "They're off! Go,
Orange!" called Antipas.

"White!" I cried, shaking Gundi's arm. "Look, White's
out in front! Are you still betting on Orange? My silver
denarius to your copper *quadrans*!"

"As you wish, Miss Salome," said Gundi.

On the racetrack, the chariots rounded the second turn.
An attendant flipped a brass dolphin on a rail to mark
the third lap. The White team had fallen behind, and Green
was just barely ahead of Orange. "Show your best, Orange!"
shouted Antipas. "Give them the whip!"

"Orange, Orange!" Herodias rose to her feet, along with the rest of the crowd. It was the final lap, with Orange and Green neck and neck.

"Go, White!" I called out, although my chosen team was now trailing by two lengths.

Just before the finish line, the Orange chariot pulled ahead of the Green. A satisfied smile spread over Antipas's face, and he bowed to Pilate. "Your steward may pay the fifty pieces of gold directly to my steward, Governor. A thousand thanks!"

Pilate scowled and said nothing. Gundi held out her hand to me, and I dropped the denarius into it. Antipas said to Herodias with a low laugh, "Did you see Pilate's face?"

The Orange charioteer, wearing the victor's laurel crown, paused before the Governor's pavilion. He raised his arm in a salute to Antipas. "Hail our patron, Tetrarch of Galilee and Perea! Hail, Lady Herodias!"

All eyes in the stadium were on the Tetrarch and his wife. Antipas acknowledged the charioteer with a wave, and Herodias also waved graciously. She turned to Antipas, her ruby earrings setting off the glow on her face.

But as Antipas looked at her, his satisfied smile faded. "My dove, there's something I've been meaning to explain to you. You understand, once we leave Caesarea and enter

Galilee, there are a few customs that the Tetrarch's wife will need to follow."

Herodias's glow faded a bit. "Customs? What does my lord mean?"

"Living in Rome, you may have forgotten that the traditional Jews have a culture of their own. My father taught me to respect that. By his simple policy of not offending Jewish customs, he avoided many uprisings. So, in public—anywhere outside our private quarters in the palace—you must cover your hair. Your dress must be modest. And you must not speak to men."

Herodias stared at him, her face ominously blank. Then she said, "I *must* do this? I *must* not do that? Am I not the wife of the ruler of Galilee and Perea?"

"There, you're taking this personally!" Antipas picked up her hand and kissed her emerald ring. "I'm the ruler himself, but I'm not free to offend the Jews, either. I don't eat pork—at least, not in front of traditional Jews. I don't put graven images on the coins of Galilee." Antipas laughed and went on in a lighter tone, "I'd forgotten that special law about the brother's wife."

"I don't see anything humorous," said Herodias.

"Let me explain, my dove. You remember Governor Pilate's remark about John the Baptizer last night? The

Baptizer was talking about a Jewish law that forbids marrying a brother's wife if he's alive. But if the brother dies, it's actually one's *duty* to marry his wife." He laughed again. "Perhaps if Herod Junior were to have an—an *accident,* the Baptizer would start praising me."

Now, it seemed, Herodias saw the joke, because her musical laugh rang out.

The next day we went to the amphitheater to see the games, and the day after that, we left Caesarea. I heard Antipas's guards grumbling about missing the rest of the games, but I was glad I wouldn't have to watch anyone else being killed. Excepting, of course, the chicken that had to be sacrificed at the Temple of Hermes, god of travel, to ensure a good journey. From Caesarea Maritima to Antipas's new city on the shore of Lake Tiberias was only a chicken's worth of a journey, two days' travel. We'd stop in Sepphoris overnight, then go on to reach Tiberias about evening on the second day.

Antipas got into a carriage with his steward, Chuza, and his secretary, Leander, so that he could go over business matters during the trip. Herodias and I were to ride in another carriage with her jewelry cases, baskets packed with her cosmetics jars, mirror, combs, and curling irons, trunks full of silks, and several jars of her favorite honeyed wine.

"Would my lady not rather have the baggage loaded on pack animals, instead of crowding her carriage?" suggested the caravan master. I thought this was a sensible idea, since there was hardly any place to stretch out my legs. But Herodias answered, "I wish to keep an eye on my belongings," and her tone did not invite further discussion.

The courtiers filled the rest of the carriages according to their rank. Antipas's soldiers, armed with swords and spears, rode before us and behind us.

As Herodias and I settled ourselves on the cushions, Herodias's maid, Iris, handed in a bag of roses. "They say we pass by some dreadful-smelling towns, my ladies."

"Oh, yes," said Herodias. "We'll need to bury our noses in something sweet." She explained to me, "The natives don't use Roman sanitation, except in the cities that the Herods built."

Herodias was still in a good mood this morning, chatting as if she'd never been angry with me over spotting her yellow silk *stola*—or was it over the way my stepfather had looked at me? "I see you're wearing the opal earrings today," she remarked. "They're a little dressy, perhaps, for traveling—but why shouldn't you enjoy them?" She smiled indulgently.

On the way out of the city Herodias pointed out the

massive arched aqueduct that brought water to Caesarea.
"My grandfather built that. As well as this road. Do you notice how smooth it is? It's as good as any Roman highway."

I was in a cheerful mood, too. Maybe Herodias was more
respectful of me after seeing me as a young woman. She reported how Antipas had instructed her to behave (she didn't
know I'd overheard at the races), quoting his words in a
pompous voice. I laughed and laughed. It was delightful to
hear her making fun of Antipas for a change instead of going
on about how wonderful he was.

"How did you like the mock battle yesterday?" Herodias
changed the subject. "Wasn't the Governor the most entertaining part of it?" She made me laugh again with her wicked
imitation of Governor Pilate, jumping up and down as he
cheered on the fighters in the amphitheater. "You'd think
that clod was the victorious general himself. Obviously he
believes his stint in the Roman army was the best time of his
life. It probably was, poor fellow."

"I felt sorry for the gladiators," I said. "Did you see the
two friends fighting back to back? They were the only ones
left against the trident wielders."

"My pet." Herodias leaned forward to stroke my cheek.
"I understand how you feel, but you need to realize that

those men in the arena are desperate criminals. They deserve to die. Do you know what helped me when I started watching the games? I pretended I was looking at a battle in a wall painting, only the figures moved. Or I'd tell myself, We in the stands are like the gods on Mount Olympus, watching mortals fight for our entertainment. The games have nothing to do with us."

I tried, just for a moment, to picture yesterday's gladiator fights the way she advised. But what flashed in my mind was the instant when one of the fighting friends crumpled to the ground, wounded. Crying out, the other gladiator bent over him. Then he, too, was struck down. The crowd cheered for the victorious trident wielders, and slaves dragged the bodies away.

I pushed the memory away, but then instead I remembered that foggy morning on the *Ceres* when Simon had disappeared. "Herodias," I said suddenly, "what really happened to Simon?"

She gave an annoyed laugh. "How your mind skips around! It was a pity about Simon, but he was such a fool, even aside from . . . He actually hinted that he'd ask for your hand in marriage if we gave him any encouragement."

Herodias had not answered my question. But before I could protest, she turned the conversation to our new life in

Tiberias. There would be boat trips on the lake, and we'd go to the theater and the spa. Tiberias had a fine marketplace, attracting traders from Gaul in the northwest of the Empire, from Babylon in the southeast, and beyond. Oh!—and especially for me, Herodias had spoken to Antipas about building a shrine to Diana.

It was pleasant to be alone with my mother, like old times, and so I didn't remind her that I was to be married off, probably far from Tiberias. In any case, Diana, protector of maidens, wouldn't be interested in me once I was married.

About mid-morning we turned off the Via Maritimus, the main trade route, and followed another road east. Parting the carriage curtains, I saw hills planted with vineyards and olive orchards and low hovels here and there. The buildings looked more like goat sheds than houses.

The hills sloped down to a broad plain covered with fields of grain. "There are some fertile farmlands in Galilee, aren't there?" remarked Herodias. "After we get settled in Tiberias, I must get Antipas to deed me my own estates or perhaps a tax revenue."

"Why?" I asked, thinking of the ruby earrings. "He gives you anything you ask for."

"Yes," she said, "but it's not the same as having one's own wealth. I lost my dowry when I left Junior, you see."

A sober note in my mother's voice made me glance at her. She was still gazing out the window, and there was a line of worry between her eyes. I felt suddenly uneasy myself, as if Herodias and I were not in a carriage, but in a little boat on the high seas. Then the moment passed. Smothering a giggle behind her hand, Herodias began to tell me some gossip about Procula, Pilate's wife.

The road crossed the plain to a river, marked by the trees that grew thickly along its banks. Soon the forward section of our caravan, including Antipas's carriage and most of the guards, disappeared into the wooded margin. Our carriage, too, followed the road into the trees. I smelled the pleasantly cool freshwater air, and finally I glimpsed the water itself through the oaks and sycamores. By this time, the other carriage was on the farther side and disappearing into the trees again.

Our carriage paused, and a guard rode up to speak to Herodias. "Lady Herodias, the ground is very soft at the river's edge. It might be well to stop here and lighten the carriage before we ford the river. We can unload the baggage, take your ladyship and her daughter across, and return for the baggage."

"Nonsense," said Herodias. "I will keep my personal baggage with me, as I ordered at the beginning."

"Just as my lady commands," said the guard, expression-less, and he rode off.

As the carriage rolled forward again, Herodias sniffed. "Antipas's men need to learn to obey orders from his lady. And to use their heads! If the carriage is too heavy, why, hitch another horse to it! That guard's horse, for—"

A severe jolt broke off Herodias's words. The carriage pitched forward, causing her to lurch toward me. I clutched at the nearest curtain, and it ripped away from the rod.

The horses whinnied, and I heard shouts and scuffling in front of the carriage. At first I thought the driver and guards were cursing because we were stuck in the mud. The next moment, the carriage was surrounded by strangers in rough clothes, shouting in Aramaic and brandishing knives. There must have been twenty of them.

One stranger in a dirty head cloth scowled through the curtainless window. He barked a command.

I shrank away. Herodias screamed, "Help! Guards!"

The stranger spoke again, this time in halting Greek. "Give riches, quick, quick!"

"He's a bandit," I said stupidly. "He wants our jewelry." Lifting my hands to my ears, I unfastened my opal earrings.

But Herodias clutched her neck, her wrists, her hands, as

if to hold on to all her jewels as long as possible, and screamed louder still. "Help! Bandits!"

As I dropped the earrings in the bandit's hand, I noticed with wonder how young he was. He couldn't have been any older than I was—he had no beard—and he looked shorter than me.

And then more guards splashed back across the river and fell on the bandits with their swords. A few of the outlaws were killed and most of the others scattered, but the guards seized the one with my earrings. Although the young bandit struggled wildly, moments later he lay facedown on the muddy ground with his arms twisted behind his back. His sleeveless coat had come off in the fight and his tunic had ripped, showing a scrawny back with shoulder blades and ribs standing out.

As suddenly as it had begun, the bandit attack was over. We rode the guards' horses across the river and waited in Antipas's carriage while the servants dug our carriage out of the mud. The bandit attack had left me shaken, but Herodias recovered almost immediately. She entertained her husband with a lively telling of the incident, in which she bravely defended our lives, our honor, and our property. I was the clown in her story, needlessly handing over my earrings. Now they were gone, of course, trampled into the mud during the fight.

Antipas laughed at Herodias's story, but then a cold look came over his face. "This should never have happened. Chuza!" He leaned out the carriage window, where Chuza and Leander stood. "Summon the captain of the guards."

I thought my stepfather was going to punish the captain for leaving our carriage so poorly protected during the fording of the river. But Antipas and the captain quickly concluded that the caravan master was to blame, for overloading Herodias's carriage. He would be dismissed as soon as the party reached Sepphoris. As for the bandit, Antipas decided not to execute him here and now, although that would have been the most convenient thing to do. "If I have a chance to interrogate him properly," promised the captain, "he'll tell us where to find the ones who got away."

"And if there's any hint of a link to the rebels, I want to know about that," said Antipas. "Or to the river preacher, John the Baptizer."

I didn't see the bandit again, but I thought about him. His face at the carriage window stuck in my mind, only now I saw the fear in his glaring eyes. Maybe he'd never robbed a caravan before. I wished—a foolish wish, of course—that somehow I could have given him my earrings *before* the bandits attacked us.

# NINE

# THE SILVER PLATTER

Late in the afternoon of the second day, our caravan crested a ridge and paused at the Tetrarch's order. Antipas beckoned as a guard handed Herodias and me down from our carriage. "Here, I'll show you a city worth seeing."

From the height we gazed down at a lake about twice the size of Lake Sabazia, north of Rome, where we used to go for holidays. The city on the near shore gleamed in the mellow light. Herodias turned from that scene to her husband with shining eyes. "My prince! Tiberias must be the most beautiful city in the world. The magnificent building with the golden roof, splendid enough to house Zeus and Hera—is that a temple?"

"That's the palace," said Antipas. "And look, in the central square, you can see a stone point above the roof of that smaller temple. That must be the obelisk I ordered; Chuza says it was delivered from Egypt while I was away. I got it for a public sundial, like the one in the Roman Forum."

"Queen" Herodias and her Bull gazed from each other to the city, well pleased. I felt lonely, with a tinge of panic. What did it matter to me how splendid Tiberias was? It wouldn't be where *I* belonged. I yearned to be back in the Temple of Diana in Rome.

At sunset we entered Tiberias, welcomed at the gates by ranks of important citizens. In the public square our procession paused in front of the obelisk, where Antipas stepped onto its base. Chuza handed Antipas a bag of coins, a herald blew his trumpet, and Antipas tossed money to the crowd of beggars below. "May the gods bless the most gracious Tetrarch!" they shouted, scrambling for the coins.

Outside the palace, servants scattered petals in front of us as we climbed the front steps. Herodias was glowing again—scenes like this must have been what she had in mind when she married the Tetrarch of Galilee and Perea.

Greeted by the housekeeper of the women's quarters, Herodias asked to be taken to her suite. The woman said, "It isn't quite ready, my lady." Reluctantly she explained that

Antipas's first wife, the Nabatean princess, had left only the day before. "She didn't believe the prince would actually set her aside. She lingered until Steward Chuza's messenger arrived from Caesarea, saying that you had landed."

I glanced uneasily at Herodias's face, which had turned pale. "The Nabatean woman 'didn't believe the prince would set her aside,' " she repeated in a dangerously quiet voice. "And why was that? Had someone told her so? *Who* told her so? Or—was the Nabatean woman stark raving mad?"

The housekeeper turned pale, too, and licked her lips. "Mad—I am sure she was mad, my lady. Yes, the signs of madness were unmistakable. We all remarked on it—oh, yes, we did. But of course nothing could be done, with the Tetrarch and Steward Chuza both away."

Nothing could be done? I wondered. Did Antipas know that the Nabatean princess had waited until the last minute to leave? Did he care?

Herodias, however, seemed calmed by the housekeeper's words. Still, she insisted on being taken to the suite. Slaves opened the double doors, revealing a spacious main room. "Not quite ready!" exclaimed Herodias. "Indeed."

The room was strewn with carpets and furs, cushions and tableware, thrown every which way. Hangings had been half torn from the walls. There was a strong smell of an aromatic spice.

"*Pee-yew!* This place stinks of coriander." Herodias stared around, as if she might find the Nabatean princess herself lurking behind a drapery. "Throw out all this trash. And scrub the floor and walls with lye."

"Throw out . . . everything, my lady?" The housekeeper's eyes widened. "These carpets are very fine Persian work, and some of the serving pieces—" She touched a silver platter on the chest by the bed.

I picked up the platter. It was round and as wide across as my shoulders. With a finger I traced the silver grapes and leaves around the edge and the silver grapevine handles.

"*Hmm,* yes," said Herodias, peering at the platter. "Very finely wrought. Well, keep anything easy to clean, like this." She stepped around the room, pointing out this piece or that to save.

I thought it was a pity to throw out the jewel-colored carpets, and I slipped off a sandal to stroke the soft pile of one with my toes. Feeling a pinch on my ankle, I slapped at a black dot.

"Fleas. I'm not surprised," said Herodias. "Burn the carpets and cushions," she instructed the housekeeper. "I'll stay in the guest suite until this place is cleansed."

As we continued our tour of the palace, Herodias seemed to have decided to treat the hasty departure of Antipas's first wife as a joke. Pausing on the highest terrace, she asked me, "Can't you imagine that desert woman scrambling out the back door to her camel?" She giggled. "Losing her sandal on the steps?"

Entering into Herodias's spirit, I stood on tiptoe at the terrace railing and pointed southward. "Look, I think I see her in the distance. There's a black trail behind her—the fleas, I guess."

"May they follow her all the way to Petra," said Herodias. She dimpled at me.

That night the Nabatean princess came to me in a dream. As I was riding in a carriage, she appeared at the window with desperate eyes and dirt-streaked face. I woke up feeling sorry for the put-aside princess, and I wished I hadn't made fun of her. Even if she had pined for her desert home in Nabatea, it was a dreadful humiliation for a wife to be put aside.

Now that the Tetrarch of Galilee and Perea was back in his capital city, he had much business to attend to, which meant that Leander had many more letters to write and records to keep. He didn't have time to give me Greek lessons every day. In fact, Antipas thought the lessons could be dropped.

But Herodias insisted that I should keep up my Greek by practicing with Leander now and then. "At least until Salome is betrothed," she cajoled Antipas. "There is nothing so winning to a man as a pretty girl reciting classical Greek poetry while she strums the lyre—don't you agree, my prince?"

Antipas laughed indulgently. "You have me there! Very well, a lesson for Salome now and then, when my secretary has time."

To my delight, Leander found time the next morning, and we met under an arbor on the lower terrace. He dutifully coached me on my emphasis and gestures, but I thought he seemed to be thinking about something else. Finally I stopped in the middle of a stanza and asked, "What is it? Are you worried about getting all your work done?"

Leander looked startled; then he sighed. "I am thinking about my work—but not about getting it done. Yesterday I read a report to Antipas from the captain of the guards in Sepphoris, about the bandit they captured at the river Kishon."

"Oh!" My dream of last night popped into my head, and I realized that the Nabatean princess at my carriage window had had the face of the young bandit. "They—they executed him?"

"Not exactly," said Leander. "The guards at Sepphoris tortured him to get the names of the other bandits and to find out where they were from. It seems that the captured bandit was from Judea, but the rest of the band were from a village just over the border in Galilee. Antipas had high praise for the captain."

I felt sick. "Why was it so important to know where they were from?" I asked.

"Because the Tetrarch has to be very careful not to offend Governor Pilate by encroaching upon his authority. So Antipas wrote—*I* wrote—the captain at Sepphoris not to execute the Judean bandit, but send him to Caesarea and hand him over to Governor Pilate's men for crucifixion. At the same time, Antipas ordered the commander of the garrison at Sepphoris to send soldiers to the other bandits' Galilean village and destroy it."

"Destroy it?" I remembered a cluster of mud huts we'd passed, where I'd noticed women at the well. "You mean, tear down the houses?" Tearing them down wouldn't take much work, I thought.

"Yes, and kill the villagers." Leander turned his pained

eyes to me. "You will say, They were bandits, and they had to be punished. Antipas had to make an example of them."

"I *wasn't* going to say that."

"But *why* had they turned to banditry?" Leander went on. "These young men had no way to live. Their families had gone into debt to pay Antipas's taxes. Then their farms were taken to pay the debts."

We were silent for a moment. I'd never thought about how bandits might become bandits in the first place. Maybe I'd thought they were born bandits, as I was born a Herod.

Leander continued the lesson, but now I was the one who couldn't keep my mind on it. I was trying not to picture the young bandit nailed up beside the Via Maritimus. I knew, of course, that the Romans crucified thieves. But I'd only seen crosses from a distance as we traveled, before Herodias pulled the carriage curtains shut.

A few days later, while we were still unpacking and settling in, Herodias sent for the court astrologer. She was pleased to have an astrologer on call, especially one trained in Babylon. "Antipas gathers only the best around him," she told me. "Your father would never pay for a first-rate astrologer like Magus Shazzar."

I'd gotten a different impression of Shazzar from Leander. Leander was too busy right now to give me another lesson, but I'd run into him once on the lower terrace. As we
chatted about this and that, Leander complained about having to eat at the same table with the astrologer. "The learned
man of Babylon has food stuck in his beard."

"But that must be a sign of his great wisdom," I said innocently. "If he wakes up hungry in the middle of the night,
he can just chew on his beard."

"True," said Leander dryly. "He could enjoy a feast without even getting out of bed."

Whether Magus Shazzar was a top astrologer or an un-
kempt swine or both, I had to wait to find out. He couldn't
attend Herodias right away, for the next day was the Sabbath, the Jewish Seventh Day. My family had never ob-
served the Sabbath, but I knew about it. In Rome, the shops
in the Jewish quarter of the city were closed every seventh
day. The Jews didn't go out on the Sabbath, except to an assembly for prayer and readings. They did no work—not
even casting an astrological chart.

Herodias was indignant that Antipas had decided to
make all his employees observe the Sabbath. "This isn't
necessary," she muttered to me. "Magus Shazzar probably

worships the Persian Mithras or some such god. Why should he observe Jewish customs?"

Herodias was still more annoyed to learn that Antipas's entire household was to begin attending the Sabbath prayer meeting. "I haven't been to one of those tedious gatherings— or wanted to—since I was a girl."

But I was curious to see the Jewish prayer meeting, and so I rose promptly on the Sabbath morning. Gundi was already up, burning a pinch of incense before her statuette of Aphrodite. We both covered our heads and shoulders, as we'd been instructed, and then we joined the rest of the court on the palace portico.

By the time we reached the assembly house, I was sweating under my wraps, for the air in Tiberias was warm and moist. We all followed Antipas up the high limestone steps and through the fluted pillars of the portico. Inside the hall, Antipas and his courtiers took their seats at the front. We women and girls were directed upstairs to the gallery.

A woman on an open litter was carried into the gallery and placed near the balustrade. "That must be the steward's wife, supposedly an invalid," remarked Herodias. "They say that Chuza converted to the Jewish religion to marry her.

What a poor bargain! Although very likely Antipas would have ordered him to convert, anyway."

We'd gotten up earlier than usual, and now I tried not to yawn as the morning went on. I longed to push the scarf off my head; I felt like a steamed fish. There were prayers, and readings from holy scrolls, and explanations of the readings. I didn't understand Hebrew, the ancient Jewish language, but the leader of the meeting translated each verse into Aramaic and Greek.

One of the prayers thanked the Lord for Prince Antipas's safe return from Rome. Beside me, Herodias seemed to be listening carefully, even as she lifted her scarf to her mouth to stifle yawns. "Why don't they give thanks for the Tetrarch's marriage?" she whispered.

I looked around at the other women and girls, and I noticed that they were eyeing Herodias and me, too. They must be the wives and daughters of the noblemen of Tiberias. I saw them glancing at Herodias's ruby earrings—she had managed to drape her head scarf so as to reveal them.

Now a rabbi, or teacher, explained an ancient text, the last words of David, a great king of ancient Israel. One passage struck me: "When one rules justly over men, ruling in the fear of the Lord, he dawns on them like the morning light . . ."

The words thrilled me, and they brought to mind Leander's

words on shipboard, "I do not admire power unless it is used in a good way." Although usually he was so composed, his voice had shook as he said this. I wished I could see Leander's face from where I was sitting. What did he think of King David's poem?

I noticed that Herodias had stopped yawning and was smiling as she watched Antipas. He listened with a satisfied expression, nodding. He seemed to think King David's poem described him. The thrill I'd felt on hearing the words faded.

After the final prayer and hymn, the other women in the gallery stood aside to let Herodias and her attendants leave first. Pausing beside the litter of the steward's wife, Herodias nodded a greeting. It was proper for Joanna, a woman of lower rank, to rise and bow to the Tetrarch's wife, and she did so. But as Joanna struggled slowly to her feet, I wished Herodias would urge her to rest on the litter.

"It is my honor to welcome Princess Herodias to Tiberias," Joanna said. I thought she looked to be about Herodias's age, maybe younger, although there were pain furrows between her eyes and lines from her nose to the corners of her mouth.

Herodias nodded in her most queenly way. "Do pay us a visit one day soon."

* * *

The day after the Sabbath, I went to the palace office to get some tablets to write a letter to a friend in Rome. I found Leander sitting at a table in the office, writing with ink on papyrus. There was a pile of silver and gold coins beside him.

Leander looked up guiltily as I came in. "Oh, Miss Salome. This isn't new papyrus," he said quickly. "I wouldn't presume to waste expensive new papyrus on a letter of my own. This is the reverse side of a business letter that the Tetrarch doesn't want to save."

"My, what a long explanation!" I teased him. "Do you really think I'd run to my stepfather and tell him you were wasting his papyrus?" I looked down at Leander's letter. "What beautiful clear script you write. I can even read it upside down. 'To my honored mother, Eustacia, from her only son—'"

"All right," said Leander, "if you must know, I'm sending my mother more money. They need it right away." He handed me a tablet, a letter from his mother.

*What do you think?* she'd written from Alexandria. *The matchmaker has arranged an excellent marriage for Chloe, with a solid citizen who has a government lease for copper mines in Lusitania. They'll sign the marriage contract as soon as we can turn over the full amount of the dowry. Oh, my dearest son, send your wages on the wings of Hermes!* At the end of the letter, she added, *We're so eager to hear everything about your life at the court of Herod Antipas.*

While I was reading, Leander had finished his own letter. He rolled up the papyrus, tied it with a string, and put it in a pouch. One by one he dropped the silver and gold coins into the pouch. The last coin was a gold aureus, and he wistfully fingered the image of Caesar Augustus stamped on it. "This alone could pay my passage back to Alexandria."

Leander sighed as he picked up a stack of parchment sheets. "Back to work. I need to take these to the palace librarian. Have you seen the library?"

I walked down the corridor with him to the room where the scrolls were stored. "These are ready for binding," he told the plump caretaker of the palace library, handing him the stack of parchment.

The librarian, another Greek, bowed to me. "Welcome, Miss Salome. I'm not a scholar, but I can tell you that my lord Antipas keeps a fine collection of written works at Tiberias. It will be my honor to assist you in finding whatever you wish." He added to Leander, "Tell me if you think of an author we ought to have. The Tetrarch wants to build up his library. He's given me permission to send to Alexandria for scrolls."

I was eager to explore the library, but right now I was

even more eager to find out what Leander was thinking, and so I left the library with him. "What is it?" I asked. "You looked like you were going to burst in there. Isn't it really a good library? There were hundreds of scrolls on the shelves."

"Oh, it's an excellent library," said Leander sourly. "It has all the world's great philosophers: Plato, Aristotle, Philo of Alexandria, and . . . Herod Antipas." A corner of his mouth pulled down. "The parchment I gave the librarian was a volume of the Tetrarch's diary."

"His Deep Thoughts?" I guessed.

"Precisely." Leander gave a groan. "I am so ashamed to take part in this fraud. I do not deserve the name of philosophy student." He glanced at me. "Do you know what he's gotten into his head now? He thinks he might be the Anointed One of the old Jewish prophecies!"

"The Anointed One?" I repeated.

"Yes, a sort of new King David who's supposed to appear and rescue the Jewish people from the conquerors. If this were a Greek tragedy, you know, the gods would strike Antipas down for his overweening pride." He snorted. "I just hope I'm not standing next to him when the thunderbolt falls."

# TEN

# A BALEFUL INFLUENCE

I spent much of my time on the highest terrace in the palace, watching for travelers approaching the city gates. It was the southern gate I was most worried about. Gundi had picked up some alarming gossip from Herodias's maid, Iris: Antipas was thinking of ways to make amends to the king of Nabatea for putting aside his daughter. To prevent the king from attacking Perea, Antipas might marry me off to the king's son.

Me, live in a flea-ridden tent in the desert! Surely Herodias wouldn't allow that . . . but I wasn't absolutely confident, after hearing Antipas instruct her in proper behavior, that he would abide by her wishes. And what would the Nabateans do to me once I was in their clutches? I had a feeling that life in Nabatea could be quite unpleasant and short for the daughter of Herodias, second wife of Antipas.

So when I spotted an important-looking caravan arriving at the south gate, I immediately sent Gundi to find out where they were from. To my relief, it turned out that they were only a party of Jewish nobles from Jerusalem. Even if one of them wanted to marry me, that couldn't be nearly as bad as a Nabatean fate.

I went cheerfully off to the market with Gundi. Since Leander's sister was to be married, I wanted to buy her a wedding present. Also, Herodias had urged me to pick out a pair of pretty earrings to replace the ones the bandit took. There *were* advantages to being the Tetrarch's stepdaughter compared with being only the daughter of stingy Herod Junior. In Tiberias, I could buy anything I liked, within reason, and the merchant would collect the price from Antipas's treasurer.

"A well-woven Persian carpet holds its value," suggested Gundi as we passed the carpet dealers' arcade.

"But it's a bulky thing to send all the way to Alexandria," I said. Still, the carpets were enticing. I stopped to admire a rack of carpets like the lovely ones my mother had ordered to be burned. Wait—this carpet was the very same pattern—

I leaned forward and sniffed the wool. A strong scent of coriander. I smiled to myself. So "Queen" Herodias thought her command was law, did she?

I returned from the market with a beautiful bronze lamp for Leander's sister as well as earrings for myself. A goldsmith had showed me opal earrings very much like the ones I'd lost, but I didn't want them after all. I chose silver ones with moonstones instead.

Back in the palace, I found that Herodias had left word for me to hurry to her rooms. Shazzar had completed her horoscope and was ready to read it. "Why not a horoscope for Miss Salome, I ask myself?" mused Gundi innocently. "*Her* whole life lies ahead of her."

I thought Gundi had a point; I was the one with the uncertain fate. I took my time about obeying Herodias's summons, although I was curious to see the astrologer work his art.

Magus Shazzar, a gray-bearded man, wore a special dark blue robe for the reading. The cloth twinkled like the night sky, with bits of glass sewed in the patterns of constellations. On a table in Herodias's sitting room, he unrolled star charts, covered with notes in a language I didn't recognize. He also set up a board inlaid with the signs of the zodiac and positioned markers on Herodias's sign, the Scorpion.

Reading the horoscope was a lengthy process. As Shazzar droned on about the houses of the different planets and the motions of the moon and the sun, I began to yawn. But not Herodias. She seemed to luxuriate in the attention from the astrologer, as if she were enjoying a massage.

When Shazzar explained Herodias's forecast for the days ahead, though, her expression darkened. He had discovered what he called a "baleful influence" in her chart. "You see, my lady, a certain man has the potential to occult your sign."

Herodias drew her breath in sharply. "I knew it! The Baptizer."

Shazzar stroked his beard, came across a bread crumb, and absently popped it into his mouth. "*Mm,* this conjunction is *very* unusual. I see that my lady also has the potential to occult him."

Herodias stared at the zodiac board as if it were a letter with bad news. "To *occult* him. To blot out this 'baleful influence.' And how may I do that—do your stars say?"

The astrologer glanced up, surprised at her tone of voice. He seemed to have forgotten that he was talking about her life. "Ah—apparently it would have to be quite a roundabout way. I will say, though, that this very day is favorable for action, for one with my lady's stars."

Later, during the midday rest, I didn't feel like napping.

Stepping quietly out the latticed doors from my room into the garden, I knelt on the edge of a fountain. I felt aimless, and I wished I could see what lay ahead for me. (If only I had known and could have taken another path!) I would ask Herodias to have the astrologer cast my horoscope.

As I trailed my fingers in the water, voices in the loggia above broke into my thoughts.

Antipas: "Still fretting about the Baptizer, my precious? What he says has nothing to do with you personally."

Herodias (doubtfully): "*Mm.* Dear heart, is it my imagination, or does that river preacher have some kind of hold over you? What can it be?" Her tone was warm and concerned.

"A hold?" said Antipas. "I wouldn't say a *hold.* An interest, perhaps. I sometimes wonder if . . ." An intense note came into his deep voice. "Is it possible that the Baptizer is a true prophet, truer than he understands himself? He preaches of a great king coming, of the dawn of a new age."

I remembered Antipas's pleased expression as he listened to the reading in the Jewish assembly hall. It was just as Leander had said: my stepfather thought that *he* could be that great king, a second King David. No wonder Leander was disgusted if he had to write down these Deep Thoughts.

"My prince," said Herodias, "surely you don't need a wandering preacher to tell you that you could be as great a king as your father? Even greater! And what does the Baptizer mean by saying that our marriage is a *sin*? Junior divorced me, and you divorced the Nabatean woman. And we consulted a soothsayer about the marriage day, and we sent offerings to all the proper gods and goddesses, including the Jewish god as I remember."

"Yes, yes," said Antipas. "We've been over all this before. I want to rest now."

"Only do away with him," said Herodias urgently, "and we'll both rest well."

"Why are you so afraid of him, my dove?" asked Antipas. "How could a penniless holy man harm the Tetrarch's wife? Besides, doing away with him would be foolish and dangerous."

"That sounds more like your cautious half brother Philip than the Prince Antipas I adore. Could it be that *you're* the one who's afraid?" Herodias laughed to show that she was joking—somewhat. "Simply give the order. You're the ruler of this land!"

Antipas's voice was like a warning rumble from a bull. "Yes, I am indeed the ruler of Galilee and Perea. I wish to remain so. Don't you remember the folly of my brother Archelaus and how it was punished? When he tried to play the grand tyrant of Judea, the Jews complained to the Emperor, and the Emperor banished him to Gaul." He went on in a lighter tone, "Believe me, exile in the northern provinces wouldn't suit you, Lady Herodias. You would not delight in weaving sensible woolen cloth and breeding chickens."

"Pooh!" Herodias made a scornful noise, as if blowing away an empty threat. Then suddenly she made her voice honey sweet. "Won't you give this one order to set my heart at peace? How many other men have been slain at your word? Why not say the word again and take care of just one more? He's not even a Roman citizen."

Antipas snorted like a bull bothered by flies. Then he said, "I don't want to talk about it anymore. I'll do this much: I'll send a messenger south to my garrison at Macherus to have the Baptizer arrested. You have to admit that he can't do any harm in a prison cell, no matter how much he preaches."

I waited to hear if my mother would insist on having the Baptizer killed. But she must have decided she'd gained as much as she could for now.

I wandered from the garden to the palace library. The librarian was taking his midday rest on a bench, so I tiptoed along the shelves. I thought I would look for some Greek poetry and surprise Leander by memorizing it.

As I was reading the tags on the scrolls, someone appeared

in the doorway. I turned, hoping it might be Leander. I was eager to give him the wedding present for his sister.

But it was Antipas. "Good afternoon, Salome," he said.

"Good afternoon, Stepfather." A vague idea came to me: if I could get Antipas to care more about me, he might consider my feelings before marrying me off. I lowered my eyelashes, raised them to meet his eyes for a moment, then swept them down again, the way Herodias did. "What a fine library you have."

He nodded, looking pleased. "The librarian was trained in Alexandria—knows his business." He stepped closer. "What are you reading?"

I could smell the perfumed oil on his beard, and I felt a little nervous. "I was just looking for—I like poetry."

"Poetry—is that so?" Antipas lifted the tag of the scroll in my hands and read the Latin title. "*The Art of Love,* by Ovid. Do you like that book?"

I was alarmed at the change in his voice and at the way he was looking at me. "I—I haven't read it."

Antipas stared at me for a moment, his tongue just showing between his teeth. "No—not yet." Dropping the tag, he strolled from the library.

When he was gone, I took the scroll from its case and unrolled it. It was in Latin, which I could read somewhat. I glanced at a verse here, a verse there, my face growing hotter and hotter. My eye lit on the line, *Out in the springy meadow the heifer lows with longing for the bull.* These poems were indecent; they were all about lust.

I must explain to Antipas that I would never read such poems. But how could I explain without bringing up the embarrassing poems themselves? Pushing the scroll back in its cubbyhole, I, too, left the library.

The next morning, Herodias was in a merry mood. Antipas's messenger was on his way to Macherus, the fortress in the south, and soon John the Baptizer would be in prison. "Of course," Herodias told me, "it would have been more sensible for Antipas to order the preacher to be killed on the spot. But one step at a time!"

After breakfast Herodias took me to pay a call on Joanna, wife of Antipas's steward. "The steward's wife ought to have come to pay her respects to me by now," remarked Herodias, "but of course she has a mysterious weakness in her limbs. Chuza works so hard for my prince," she added sweetly. "We must be kind to his ailing wife."

The steward's house on the palace grounds was not large, but I thought there was something harmonious and peaceful about it. In the central hall, wooden screens let in lemon-scented air from the garden. Joanna greeted us from her couch, where she half reclined, propped up by cushions. The lines of pain in her face looked deeper than they had on the Sabbath.

"Please excuse me for not rising," said Joanna in a soft voice. "My malady comes and goes, always leaving me a little weaker. Today it's upon me. But it's so kind of your ladyship and her daughter to visit. How do you like Tiberias? They say our city is a bit like Napoli in Italy, built on the hillside overlooking the water."

Herodias agreed and went on to praise the palace. She added, "Of course there's so much redecoration to do in my suite. The Nabatean woman had it looking like the inside of a tent!"

The steward's wife smiled faintly. "Yes, the poor girl seemed to be homesick. . . ." She turned to me. "So, Salome. That's a name to be proud of in your family. Your ancestor Salome, sister of Herod the Great, was bold and merciful. You must know the story of how she spared the Jewish leaders at his death?"

"Of course," said Herodias before I could answer. "Although my Salome is hardly like my great-aunt!" She looked at me with fond amusement. "Now *that* Salome—she was a woman to be reckoned with."

I said nothing, but I didn't like the way Herodias was talking about me. Wasn't there any chance that *I* might be a woman to be reckoned with? Actually, although I did know the story Joanna mentioned, I'd never heard it told in praise of Salome. Rather, the point of the story was always what a bloodthirsty tyrant King Herod had been to the very end of his life. While he lay on his deathbed, my great-grandfather had worried that the Jews would rejoice instead of mourn when they heard the news of his death. (Who could have blamed them?)

So Herod ordered all the Jewish leaders arrested and kept in the stadium. As soon as the king died, his soldiers were to kill the leaders. Thus, Herod planned, the Jewish people would be forced to mourn his death. But when the king actually did breathe his last, Salome hastened to the captain of the guards and stopped him from carrying out the executions.

"And wasn't there also another ancestor, Salome Alexandra," Joanna went on, "called Queen Alexandra?"

"Indeed," said Herodias, pleased. This was just what she'd reminded me of before we left Rome. "She ruled Judea before the Herods took power."

"She's an ancestor to be proud of, too," said Joanna. "Queen Alexandra kept the peace in her lifetime, which I think was harder than winning great battles."

I looked at Joanna with curiosity and respect. I hadn't expected the steward's wife to be so well informed or to have her own opinion about what was admirable in rulers.

"How knowledgeable the steward's wife is about the past!" Herodias echoed my thought. "But to tell the truth, I'm more interested in the present. You know, Galilee may be very scenic in its way, but I didn't expect so much—well, *unrest*. The bandits that attacked our caravan between Caesarea and Sepphoris . . . the religious fanatics roaming the countryside, agitating the peasants . . ."

A while later, as Herodias and I walked back to the palace, she gave a little laugh. "No, I don't think there's much wrong with the steward's wife. I think she's found a good way to get special attention. I'll have to remember that ploy if I ever lose my looks."

A few days later, Herodias and I tried the famous hot springs outside the city. While Herodias was having a massage, I went to soak in the warm pool. The steward's wife was already there, chatting with another woman, the wife of a courtier. I slipped into the pool without disturbing them.

"Thank you for asking, Dorcas; the healing waters do me good," Joanna was saying. The lines in her face seemed softened. "I believe I've taken a turn for the better."

"I hope so," said the other woman.

I, too, hoped that Joanna had taken a turn for the better, because there was something I liked very much about her. Clean and comfortable, I thought. That seemed like an odd way to describe a person's spirit. But it *was* the feeling she gave off, the way the lemon tree in her garden gave off a fresh, sweet scent.

"Did the holy man grant you a healing?" Dorcas was asking Joanna.

"No . . ." Joanna sounded puzzled. "I know that's why I went to see him. But when I was actually in his presence, my illness didn't seem important."

"I don't understand," said Dorcas. "You've been burdened with this mysterious malady for how long? Almost three years!"

I didn't understand, either, but I was curious. I tried to look like I wasn't listening. Leaning my elbows on the edge of the pool, I gazed up at the vaulted ceiling. A bird flew through the baths, its wing beats echoing.

"Yes, yes," said Joanna, "but the hardest thing about being ill isn't the pain or the weakness. It's having to think about myself so much. When I listened to the holy man, suddenly I wasn't thinking about myself at all. He opened a window on a new world."

"And what did you see out that window?" asked her friend.

"I saw other people, struggling and suffering. I never noticed them before, but they're all around us, people as real as you or me. Jews, Syrians, Greeks, Samaritans . . . I saw that by selling just one of my properties, I could make an enormous difference for them."

"Selling your *property*?" exclaimed her friend. (I was startled, too.) "Oh, Joanna, what are you saying? Don't do anything rash! You already give alms to beggars. You and Chuza give the required amount for the Jewish poor, don't you? No one could expect any more than that."

I sneaked a glance at Joanna, curious to see what she would answer.

"But I expect more now that my eyes are opened. Dorcas, if you could have heard the holy man! I'm so impatient to turn my life around. Then I could go south again to be cleansed in the—"

Dorcas interrupted, clearing her throat loudly. *"Joanna."* She had noticed me. Now Joanna turned and recognized me, too.

"I'm sorry," I said, embarrassed. "I didn't mean to eavesdrop." What a feeble lie! I started to pull myself out of the pool, then changed my mind and slid under the surface. I held my breath as long as I could.

When I came up again, Dorcas was out of the pool, wrapped in a towel, and leaving the warm room with her maid. But Joanna, still in the water, watched me thoughtfully with her head on one side. I gave her a sheepish smile.

"Salome," said Joanna. She paused. "Can you imagine a window opening on a new world?"

I'd tried to put my dream in the Temple of Diana out of my mind, as if it were a childhood toy. But now, at Joanna's words, the dream burst into my mind as vivid as the night I dreamed it. "Oh, yes!"

Joanna seemed surprised at my response, but her face broke into a smile. She looked at me, smiling without speaking, for a long moment.

I wanted to ask her if her "holy man" was the same person as John the Baptizer. I wanted to find out if the desert preacher gave Joanna the same feeling I'd had when Diana chose me.

But the moment was over. Joanna nodded goodbye to me and signaled her maid to help her out of the pool. I was left soaking in the warm water and my stew of thoughts. I wondered if I should tell Herodias about this conversation. For I was almost sure that the preacher who had inspired Joanna to "turn her life around" *was* the same man that Herodias wanted dead.

# ELEVEN

# JOHN ARRESTED

Antipas's soldiers, a squad of them, appeared at John's camp after midnight. Elias was on guard outside the cave, but he scarcely had time to shout a warning before a soldier knocked him down with the butt of his spear.

"Baptizer!" barked the officer. "Come out before we smoke you out like a jackal!"

John stepped out of the cave. "I am John, called the Baptizer."

At a nod from the officer, two soldiers seized his arms. Ignoring the disciples scrambling out of the cave, they turned and hustled John uphill toward the road. They must be taking him to Macherus.

Not now, John protested silently. Not so soon.

He'd known this moment would come, and he thought he'd accepted that. But now John seemed to see Antipas's grim fortress Macherus looming before him, and he had to restrain himself to keep from resisting. He must not fight; if he did, his disciples would fight for him, and they would be hurt.

But the people who were counting on him—what about them? The throngs would arrive at the riverbank as soon as it was light. Some of them would come to hear John's message for the first time. Some, having spent weeks following a new way of life, were ready to be baptized. All those hopeful faces, with the hope draining out of them. What would become of those people now?

As the group reached the highway, John became aware of something odd about the way the guard on the left held his arm. Something hesitant. Turning sideways, John looked at the man's face. The guard stared stubbornly ahead, but even in the flickering torchlight, John could see that he was miserable. And John recognized him—this was the same soldier who had come a few days ago with the warning.

# TWELVE

# A DANGEROUS MAN

One morning not long after meeting Joanna at the hot springs, I heard shouting outside the south gates. Not the Nabateans, come to bargain for me! I ran to the edge of the terrace.

The sun, just above the bluffs on the other side of the lake, shone on a troop of Antipas's blue-caped soldiers. They escorted a man in rough clothing, with untrimmed hair and beard. His hands were chained in front of him.

"So you got the Baptizer," called out a guard from the gate tower.

"We always get our man," answered the captain. The

gates clanged open, and the men tramped under the arch and disappeared.

I gasped. I could hardly believe Antipas had done this to Herodias. She thought the desert preacher was safely locked up far away in Macherus. What would she say when she found out? I was a little fearful of Herodias's anger. At the same time, I hoped she'd now realize that Antipas couldn't be trusted.

I hurried to Herodias's suite, where her maid told me she was still asleep. Iris insisted on waking her mistress in a special way. Rubbing a feather with perfumed ointment, she waved it near Herodias's nose. A dreamy smile appeared on her face, and her eyes fluttered open.

"Why, Salome," she said, catching sight of me at the foot of her bed. She stretched and sighed. "Do you know, I like living in Tiberias. I thought I'd miss Rome, but this city is like a little Rome." She gave a girlish giggle. "Except that I'm like a queen here—queen of Galilee and Perea and—later, who knows!"

She had no idea what Antipas had done. Or—had *she* persuaded Antipas to bring the Baptizer here, to execute him?

When I told her what I'd seen, her dreamy mood vanished. "What! Antipas promised—" Throwing off the blanket, she jumped out of bed. Iris nervously held out clothes for her to put on.

"How could he do this?" Herodias exclaimed. Flinging her arms around, she stuck herself on a brooch, screamed, and slapped her maid. Iris held out a comb, but Herodias stormed off toward the Tetrarch's suite with her hair all wild.

She was soon back, though. The Tetrarch had left the palace early with his steward, she'd found out. It seemed that Antipas was inspecting the site for the new shrine to Diana. He'd return later this morning for his weekly public audience, and he'd ordered the Baptizer to be brought before him. "You can be sure I'll be there, too," added Herodias.

Herodias had me stay in her rooms to keep her company while her maid was arranging her hair and patting her face with powder. "So I was right! The preacher does have some kind of hold over Antipas. He wants to *talk* to the man!"

As Herodias went on and on, I began to feel as tense as a lyre string pulled too tight. To distract myself, I opened her jewelry chest and fiddled with the gold chains and bangles. The emerald ring caught my eye, and I slipped it on my finger.

Herodias had stopped talking. I glanced up at her. One of her eyes was lined with kohl, but the other was not yet made up, which gave her a slightly deranged look. In a low tone she said, *"Take off my engagement ring."*

Hastily I put Herodias's ring back in the chest. Muttering something about getting ready for the audience myself, I slipped out of the room.

Gundi thought that Prince Antipas would hold his audience in the main hall, but I'd gotten the impression, from something Herodias had said, that the audience would take place in the great formal courtyard. With Gundi grumbling along behind me (mainly in her Germanic tongue, but with enough Greek words thrown in for me to catch her meaning), I hurried to the public end of the palace and down a flight of broad steps to the courtyard.

But the grand dais at the far end of the courtyard was empty. The only people in sight were a man at the outer gate, the younger man with him, and two guards blocking their way. "Get out of here," said one of the guards to the men. "The Tetrarch doesn't want to be bothered with your stories of figs and olives."

"Justice is justice," said the older man. He was dressed in a coarse but decent robe, and he leaned on a walking staff. "That's what the Tetrarch's public audience is for. I have a right to stand before my prince in public court and appeal for justice."

"It's Prince Antipas's client who seized our orchards!" added the younger man. "Who else should my father appeal to if not the Tetrarch?"

The guards burst out laughing. "You old fool!" said the second guard to the father. "If *Antipas's* client took your orchards and you appeal to *Antipas,* how do you think he'll decide the case?" He turned to the first guard, dropping his jaw and rubbing his chin in mock stupidity. They both guffawed again.

"Anyway," the first guard added, "the Tetrarch is holding court in the main hall, not here." (Gundi raised her eyebrows at me in a silent I-told-you-so.) "No, commoners can't walk through the palace to the hall. Go around outside if you're dead set on trying to get a hearing."

"But be ready to get a kick in the backside instead," remarked the second guard.

The old farmer's shoulders sagged, and he turned to go. But his son noticed me. "Lady—gracious lady! You must have some influence at court."

I shook my head, backing away.

"If only you would help us get a hearing!" pleaded the young man. "That's all we ask for, a—"

One of the guards took a threatening step toward the

young farmer, and he broke off. I turned and scurried out of the courtyard.

As Gundi and I made our way through the palace to the hall, I brooded over the young farmer's words. I didn't think of myself as a lady, though I supposed I was one. But why had the man appealed to *me*? Why would he think I had any influence?

Come to think of it, the idea of influence had crossed my own mind when I was talking to Antipas in the library. I blushed. But that was quite different, because I'd thought of getting a personal favor.

I entered the main hall, where the rest of the court was already in attendance. Many other people, including the ones I'd seen at the Jewish prayer meeting, crowded the majestic room. As an official seated me on a bench near the dais, Joanna was carried to a place near the front. If her "holy man" *was* John the Baptizer, I thought, she must be as upset as Herodias that he was here. Upset for a different reason, of course.

Leander stood to one side of the dais, note tablet and stylus ready. Herodias sat beside Antipas, both her eyes now made up and the emerald ring firmly on her finger. She wore her "Queen Herodias" expression, but a tense muscle twitched in her jaw.

Antipas didn't seem aware of his wife, although she was right next to him. Intent and eager, his gaze returned again and again to the back of the hall. For just an instant, his eyes rested on me, and his expression changed. He was still intent, but more like a hunting dog pointing at a pheasant. I looked away.

Then a courtier bent down to whisper to Antipas. The Tetrarch nodded, and the man called to the back of the hall, "Bring the prisoner in!" The crowd parted down the middle to let two guards through, pulling the Baptizer along by his elbows toward Antipas's throne.

I glanced at Herodias, wondering if she now felt foolish for being afraid of this man. His wrists were still chained. Next to the brawny guards, he looked underfed and not very tall. With his coarse camel-hair tunic and weathered face, the famous prophet might be mistaken for a shepherd.

Herodias looked puzzled, but not reassured. As the Baptizer came closer to Antipas's throne, I thought, He's not acting like a humble commoner seeing the inside of a palace for the first time. He didn't seem to notice the splendid scarlet columns to either side of him, or the intricate mosaic floor under his rough sandals, or the well-dressed crowd staring at him. John kept his eyes straight ahead, on the Tetrarch. Stopping before the dais, he didn't bow to Antipas, but looked up at him through matted hair.

"Well, John Baptizer?" said the Tetrarch. "I hear you have a message for me."

"Yes. I have a message for you, Antipas, and for all the Lord's people." John's voice was much stronger than I expected from this scrawny man. He hadn't addressed my stepfather as "Prince Antipas," I noted, or "Tetrarch," or even "my lord." Was he so unmannered, or did he dare to address the ruler of Galilee and Perea as an equal?

Turning from one side of the court to the other, the desert preacher let his voice ring out even louder, filling the hall. "Repent! Turn from evil. Prepare for the coming of the Lord's anointed." He seemed aware, for the first time, of all the embroidered robes and gold necklaces in the crowd. "If you have two coats, share with the person who has none." As his eagle's gaze neared me, I felt uncomfortable, and I pulled my silk *palla* closer around my shoulders.

This man was looking at me, and Herodias, and Antipas—at all the men and women of high position here—as if we were ordinary people! Antipas, the Baptizer seemed to say by his manner, did not deserve respect for being ruler of Galilee and Perea. The one really important question about the Tetrarch was whether he was *righteous*.

Antipas made an impatient gesture. "Evil—yes, yes. What I meant was, I want to hear you prophesy." Herodias

clenched and unclenched her hands on the carved arms of
her seat, but Antipas didn't seem to notice. "Baptizer, you
call yourself a prophet—what prophecies do you have for
me?" The Tetrarch leaned forward from his throne.

"I have never called myself a prophet," answered John.
"But anyone who reads Scripture will find a prophecy meant
for the rulers of the Jews today. Hear the words of the
prophet Amos: 'Because you trample on the poor and take
from them levies of grain, you have built houses of hewn
stone, but you shall not live in them; you have planted pleasant vineyards, but you shall not drink their wine.' "

I could hardly believe my ears. This underfed, ragged
man was standing up to Herod Antipas, ruler of Galilee and
Perea, shoving the truth into his face like a torch at a wild
boar. I felt a frightening but thrilling vertigo, as if I were back
on board the ship, poised at the top of a huge wave. Glancing toward Joanna, I saw her sit up in her litter. Her face
shone. As for Leander, he stared at John as if he saw a
demigod.

A silence followed John's words, broken by Herodias's
voice. "My lord Antipas, is this dignified—holding an audience
with a homeless preacher? Why should the Tetrarch of Galilee
and Perea care what this flea-bitten, dried-up fellow thinks?"

Waving at his wife as if she were a horsefly, Antipas

leaned forward to speak again to the Baptizer. But John spoke first. "If you would rule the Jews—"

A courtier broke in. "*If* Prince Antipas would rule. Perhaps we're mistaken—is it you who rule, Baptizer? That must be why you're in chains and Prince Antipas sits upon the throne." Laughter ran around the hall, but the Tetrarch frowned and held up a hand for silence.

"Antipas"—John's voice cut through the noise—"don't deceive yourself. You presume to rule the Jews, the people of the Lord. Yet you live by the law of Rome rather than the Law of Moses. The Law of Moses says, 'You shall not covet your neighbor's wife. You shall not commit adultery.' If you truly wish to repent, put aside this woman, your brother Herod's wife."

I heard gasps, including my own, around the hall. The preacher had said it to Antipas's face, in the presence of Herodias and all the court. "This woman," he dared to call my mother. To the Baptizer, there was no difference between the poor farmer I'd seen at the palace gate and Herodias, descendant of Herod the Great and the proud Hasmonean dynasty.

Herodias had been sputtering, struggling to speak, and now she found her tongue. "Shut his mouth!"

The guards looked from Herodias to Antipas with raised

eyebrows, waiting for his order. Why did Antipas hesitate? What was going through his mind? Stroking his beard, he gave a sigh. Finally he told the guards, "That's enough. Put him in the dungeon until he can show some respect."

As the guards marched the Baptizer away down the rows of scarlet pillars, the preacher's voice boomed around the audience hall. "I respect only the word of the Lord and those who obey it."

After the audience, I was glad that Herodias shut herself up in her suite with a fierce headache. I didn't want to eat lunch with her while she ranted on about John.

The person I was itching to talk to was Leander. Hadn't the Baptizer acted out this morning what Leander had said? *I do not admire power unless it is used in a good way.*

But surely the Baptizer couldn't be allowed to speak that way about the ruler of the land. If common people could criticize the Tetrarch, who would obey his laws? What did Leander think? I thought I would soon find out, because we were to meet for a lesson today. But after lunch, as I was about to leave for the lower terrace, a slave delivered a note from Leander: Antipas wanted his secretary's services this afternoon after all.

If I couldn't talk to Leander, I decided, I'd go see Joanna.

Maybe I could find out why her face had lit up as she listened to the desert preacher. She wouldn't talk freely to me, Herodias's daughter, about John, but still I was curious to see what she would say. I sent Gundi to the steward's house to ask if Joanna would receive a visitor.

I thought Joanna might be tired out from going to court, but Gundi grudgingly reported that the steward's wife would be glad to see Miss Salome. "Aren't you afraid of catching her wasting illness?" Gundi asked me as we walked through the palace grounds. "Besides, it's midday rest time."

"You're the one who wants a nap," I told Gundi, stopping outside the door of the steward's house. "Go on back. Joanna's maid can escort me home."

I was glad to enter the steward's modest house again. Today Joanna was in the garden, and she beckoned me in. It was a small garden, but pleasant, with cushions on the benches and flowering vines twining around the pillars.

Joanna sat upright in a wicker armchair near the blossoming lemon tree. "Sit down and tell me about Rome, Salome. Do you miss your life there?"

I felt a little shy, because I wasn't used to talking about myself. But as I described my class at the Temple of Diana, Joanna seemed truly interested. I'd never told anyone except Herodias about my dream that last night in the Temple, but now I struggled to explain it to Joanna. "I was so excited and so afraid at the same time! It was like—well, like what you said at the hot springs: a window opened on a different world."

Joanna's face tightened, and she moved uneasily, but I plunged ahead. "The preacher you went to hear was John the Baptizer, wasn't he?"

Looking down at the garden path, Joanna spoke in a careful tone. "Some would say that the Baptizer is possessed by a demon. This morning, he didn't seem to notice that he was in a palace, not on the riverbank. And he insulted Antipas to his face, as though he didn't know he could be put to death for it."

"He does seem possessed, in a way," I said. "Why does he hate my mother so much?"

"You mean, why does he urge the Tetrarch to put her aside?" asked Joanna slowly. "I'm not sure he *hates* her."

"But doesn't he understand how it would ruin her life if Antipas divorced her? It would be a terrible humiliation. What would she do? Where would she go? She'd have to beg some relatives to take her in."

"Rather like what happened to the Nabatean princess," said Joanna, almost too softly to hear. Without waiting for a response from me, she gestured to her maid. "But I'm forgetting about hospitality! Zoe, bring us a cool drink. Miss Salome must be thirsty." She smiled politely. "And after refreshments, I'm afraid, I must rest, or I will suffer tomorrow for overextending myself."

I was the one who'd overextended myself, of course. I shouldn't have mentioned John the Baptizer by name. Sipping my drink, I meekly went back to chatting about life in Rome. An unpleasant possibility struck me: maybe Joanna suspected that Herodias had sent me to pump her about the preacher.

Joanna must have liked me anyway, though, or maybe she just didn't want to hurt my feelings. As I was about to leave, she said, "Please come to see me again, Salome. Do you know any poetry? I'd enjoy hearing it."

I returned to the palace puzzling over what Joanna had said, or hinted at, about my mother. Although I'd been very angry with Herodias for marrying Antipas, it had never occurred to me that it might be *wrong* for her to do so.

# THIRTEEN

# A VISIT FROM HEROD ANTIPAS

Outside the audience hall, the guards marched John quickly through the palace to the back stairs. Here the magnificence came to a sudden end, and rough stone steps led downward to the prisons. There was no light except from the lamps flickering on the walls. The jailer let them through an iron gate, and the guards shoved John along the passageway, past the cell where he'd been kept this morning.

Another stairway, narrower than the first. John was afraid he might suffocate. It wasn't the prison air, although that was stale and foul. He felt as if the stones of the prison walls were pressing on him, weighing more with each step downward.

Finally the forward guard stopped, holding his torch to show a grate in the stone floor. The other guard lifted up the iron grating with a crowbar and jerked his head from John to the hole. The torch didn't light the pit except for its rim, but John found that it wasn't as deep as it looked. In fact, it wasn't deep enough for him to stand upright.

With a scraping noise, the grate dropped back into place overhead.

Facing Antipas in the grand hall, John had felt as strong and sure as an avenging angel. Now he struggled like a drowning man in a lake of dread. Hell, Gehenna, was supposed to be a land of eternal fire, but John thought this cell would be a much worse place of punishment.

John tried to escape from the prison by turning his thoughts to the outside world: the arch of sky over the hills, the gurgle of the creek flowing into the baptizing pool, the scent of green things growing by the river. But from prison, the wide world seemed far away and not quite real. Herod Antipas, like an evil magician, had shrunk John's world down to a box of clammy stone.

Torchlight flickered overhead, and John braced himself for a soldier with a drawn sword. Instead, when the guard pried up the grating, John's disciple Elias peered down. "Rabbi?"

John raised his manacled hands to grasp his disciple's. "Peace, Elias! Thank the Lord." With his friend here, John could even smile. "You made good time from Jericho to Tiberias."

John didn't ask how he'd gotten into the prison, but Elias muttered, "A friend, a wealthy lady, gave the guards silver." His breathing was labored, and he stared down at John with anxious eyes.

"Don't worry. I'm well, Elias," said John. It calmed him to reassure his disciple. "Give me the news. Where are the others?"

"Rabbi, we're all staying with good people in the next town, Capernaum." Elias hesitated. "They tell us your cousin Yeshua is preaching nearby, in Nain. Crowds are following him around. Many say that he's the prophet Elijah come back to life."

"Yeshua?" The last time John had seen his cousin, Yeshua had been in a group at the river, waiting to be baptized. The mood at baptisms was always thrilling, but there had been a special breathless feeling about that day. After the immersion, Yeshua had disappeared before John had a chance to speak to him.

"Some even say he's the Anointed One," said Elias, "come to rescue the Lord's people."

A tremor of hope shook John's heart. He answered, "Maybe he is the One. What does *he* say about himself?"

Elias shrugged and shook his head.

If the One for whom John had prepared the way was here, then the Baptizer's work was done. The Lord's purpose was going forward. In spite of the way it seemed, the Herods were not in control. This luxurious palace, squatting on its own filth, was not the real center of power.

"Go to Yeshua and ask him," John urged. "Ask him outright. Say, 'Your kinsman John wants to know, are you the Messiah? Or should we look for someone else?' Then come back and tell me what he says."

After Elias left, doubt and despair came rushing back over John. "Weakling!" he reproached himself. It wasn't the dark he minded or going hungry and thirsty. From his years in the wilderness, waiting for the word of the Lord, he was used to watching through the night and used to fasting. And he'd slept on stones many times before, in caves no larger than this cell. But those caves had opened onto the Lord's wide world.

John prayed that he would not go mad. He chanted a psalm: "My soul waits for the Lord more than watchmen for the morning, more than watchmen for the morning."

John dreamed, and in the dream angels carried him to

the wilderness. Standing on a hilltop, he breathed dry, herb-scented air. Insects hummed in the grass, and John could see the far horizon in every direction.

The day after the audience, they moved John from the pit into an ordinary cell. Here gray light trickled down from an air shaft near the ceiling. Had they moved him in preparation for executing him? John wondered. A soldier wouldn't have room to swing his sword in the pit.

Time passed. A guard unlocked his cell and set down bread and water. More time passed until the gray light faded to black again. As John was saying his evening prayers, torch-light flickered in the corridor, and the cell door opened again.

"John Baptizer," said a voice as rich as creamy cheese. "I want to talk to you."

John thought he recognized that voice, but still he squinted in disbelief at the man in the doorway. Pushing himself to his feet, John faced Herod Antipas. The Tetrarch gave off the scent of costly perfume, more frightening than the stench of the prison.

"I thought we could speak frankly, here in private," said Antipas. "It was a mistake to bring you into the audience hall yesterday. Before my court, I had to uphold my role as Tetrarch, and of course your followers were also watching you." He chuckled. "Oh, yes, I know there are servants and even courtiers who follow the Baptizer. I know that my steward's own wife traveled all the way to Jericho to hear you preach. Chuza actually believed her story about going to visit her aunt in Jericho!"

By the torchlight John noted Antipas's build, overfed but muscular, like a boar. The royal pig, thought John, that eats the flesh of the children of the poor.

"Understand," Antipas went on, "I don't argue with much of what you preach. I hear that you advise soldiers and tax collectors about how to behave better. This is good, John; this is good. But you've spoken very harshly of me."

"I've said only, turn from evil," said John. "He who would rule the Lord's people must become clean himself."

"Evil! Can you call it *evil,* John, that I've saved Galilee and Perea from Roman rule?" Antipas stretched out a hand, appealing to the preacher as one reasonable man to another. "Wasn't it a great accomplishment of mine to keep Galilee an independent territory? If it weren't for my connections in Rome, Galilee as well as Judea would be under Governor Pilate's thumb. You remember how Pilate tried to defile the Temple with the Imperial standards when he arrived in Jerusalem."

"*You* have defiled the tombs of the Jews to build this wicked city," said the Baptizer.

"If you want to talk of evil—well! The true evil is that I was cheated out of the throne of Greater Judea. My father had appointed *me* heir to his whole kingdom." The Tetrarch's tone was hurt. "But then the old man went senile, changed his mind, and gave half of his kingdom to my incompetent brother Archelaus. Archelaus made a mess of ruling Judea, the Emperor sent him into exile—and the Roman governors have been oppressing Judea ever since."

"*You* are the oppressor," said John quietly.

Folding his arms, Antipas fixed John with a reproachful look. "Baptizer, you accuse me unjustly. Why do you stir the people up against me? Why are you making life hard for me? Do you think my lot is so easy?"

When John didn't answer, Antipas went on, "It is *not* easy to rule Galilee. Think about this: I have to collect taxes for the Romans. I have to stay on good terms with the Jewish leaders. I have to keep the peasants quiet. *And* I have to watch the southern border—the king of Nabatea would like to grab a chunk of Perea. All this, with the Emperor's regent looking over my shoulder!"

"Why are you telling me these things?" asked John. "All I care about is preaching the word of the Lord. All the Lord cares about is repentance."

Antipas regarded him silently for a moment. Now,

thought John, the Tetrarch would call for the guard. He would have this troublesome preacher killed right then and there.

But Antipas said, "Very well, I never said I wouldn't repent. What must I do to repent?"

John was stunned. Was it possible that the tyrant really wanted to repent? One thing he knew: it was not up to him, John, to decide who was truly repentant. His mission was only to call the people to turn their lives around. The Lord alone could judge them.

Antipas went on, "John, let us not be enemies." He lowered his voice. "I wouldn't say this to everyone, but my fiftieth birthday coming up is making me think—how do I want future generations to remember me? The time to act is *now*. I have the official position, but you have sway over the common people. If you and I join together, Baptizer, we can make the ancient prophecies come true."

"Then listen, here is the prophecy you should heed," said John. "Hear the words of the prophet Ezekiel: 'Ho, shepherds of Israel who have been feeding yourselves! Should not shepherds feed the sheep? You eat the fat, you clothe yourselves with the wool, you slaughter the fatlings, but you do not feed the sheep.' "

Antipas sighed. "Think over what I've said." In an

abruptly cold tone he added, "And think about this: if I order it, they'll take you to the amphitheater and feed you to the panthers."

John said calmly, "The Tetrarch has no more idea of repenting than a pig." Turning his back on Antipas, he knelt on the floor, closed his eyes, and recited a psalm: "Hear, O Lord, when I cry aloud . . ."

"Consider carefully," said Antipas.

"Give me not up to the will of my enemies . . ."

"Think it over." The Tetrarch's footsteps faded in the corridor, but his perfume lingered.

# FOURTEEN

# JOANNA'S DAUGHTER

Herodias and Antipas weren't cooing and billing like turtle-doves any longer. Gundi said that Iris said that the Tetrarch didn't come to Herodias's rooms every night. When he did, they sometimes quarreled. On those nights, the visit would end with Herodias in hysterical tears and Antipas stalking back to his suite. Iris kept a sleeping potion ready every evening in case things turned out badly and her mistress needed it.

Gundi also reported that Antipas's taster said that the prison guards said that the Tetrarch had gone to the prison once, late at night. He hadn't let anyone accompany him down the stone steps, but the guards guessed that he spoke with the Baptizer.

Gundi was pleased about these setbacks for Herodias, but it worried me to hear about them. Galilee seemed more than ever like a foreign and dangerous land, and Rome seemed very far away.

I was eager to get away from the uneasy mood in the palace, and so I soon returned to Steward Chuza's house. Remembering Joanna's suggestion, I brought a collection of poems from the palace library.

As Joanna's maid Zoe led me toward the garden, I heard voices. In front of Joanna's couch knelt several people in shabby clothes, reaching out to kiss her hand. "My lady," said a fisherman, "I was about to sell my boat and hire out as a day laborer. We would have had to move to the slum outside the city walls."

"Dear lady, we owe you our lives," sobbed a young woman holding a baby. Two older children clung to her skirt. "May Hera bless you and all your family, kind lady."

"And the Jewish god, of course—may he bless you, too!" added another man.

Joanna glanced across the garden as I entered, but she hardly seemed to notice me. "Peace, farewell," she murmured to the commoners backing away from her. There were tears in her eyes.

As the young woman with the baby turned, I noticed that she looked even younger than I'd thought. Could these be her own children? Maybe she was the oldest of a family of orphans.

The commoners left, pausing again and again to look back as if they could hardly bear to take their eyes off Joanna. I sat down in a chair near her couch. "You must have sold some property," I said.

Joanna nodded, wiping her eyes. "I only wish I'd done it long ago. I didn't realize how far I'd drifted from the heart of the Law since I married. Chuza became a Jew, and of course he follows the forms and customs just as the Tetrarch demands. But that's all—there's no heart to it in Tiberias." Pausing, Joanna frowned and cleared her throat, as if she'd talked too freely. "Enough of this. I'm glad to see you, Salome. Did you bring some poetry?"

"I don't understand about the Law," I said, ignoring her question. "What *is* the heart of it?"

"To love the Lord and to love your neighbor," said Joanna. "And in order to love my neighbors, I have to notice them, don't I? It's not enough to give the alms collector a tenth of my income, as if I were paying a customs official. The holy man was telling me to open my eyes and really see the people who needed my help. How can I explain it?" She looked at me earnestly. "Imagine if you stood on the shore of Lake Tiberias, but you always turned away from the water."

I shook my head, bewildered. "How could I live in Tiberias and not look at the lake?"

"Exactly what I ask myself!" exclaimed Joanna. "Anyway, I asked the holy man what I should do to repent. He told me, 'Share your riches with the poor.' "

"Riches? But your husband is only a steward," I said.

"Yes, that's just what I thought. What riches?" Joanna gestured around her modest garden. "Then I considered the properties my father deeded to me when I married, and I saw how much more I had than I needed. And I saw people who truly needed the money." Joanna smiled sadly. "I didn't have to look far. Did you know how many farmers and fishermen in Galilee lose their means to make a living? Or how many women are widowed and left with little children to feed?"

"But there are so many poor people," I said. "How could you help them all? And what about the preacher? Did you give him money, too?"

"No," said Joanna. She looked at me as if she'd just

remembered whose daughter I was. "Later, I managed to give him some food, but that's all. I don't think he wants money." Changing the subject, she asked, "Did you notice the young widow with three little children? She reminded me a bit of my daughter."

"You have a daughter?" I asked. I thought Joanna meant a daughter who had married and left home. "Where is she?"

Joanna didn't answer at first, and I knew I must have guessed wrong. Finally she said, "My daughter died of childbirth fever—her first child. Never mind, Salome; it happened three years ago." She added in a low voice, "Although at the time, I wished I could have died in her place."

"I am so sorry," I murmured. I felt her sorrow keenly. If I had died and Herodias said she wished she could have died in my place, I would have thought, There goes the queen of tragedy again. But when Joanna said she'd wanted to die instead of her daughter, it sounded like a simple matter of fact. A question burst out of me: "Do I remind you of your daughter—a little bit?"

"Ah, Salome." Joanna reached out a hand to me, and I knelt in front of her couch, where the poor young widow had knelt a short while ago. Joanna pressed my hand between both of hers. "Dear Salome."

I seemed to sink into her words, melting as in a warm pool. I wanted more than anything for Joanna to go on talking to me in just that tone of voice. At the same time, I felt that I had no right to listen. What would Herodias think?

Joanna said gently, "No, you aren't much like Althea, my daughter, except that she was about your age." Feeling a pang, I pulled back. Joanna added quickly, "For one thing, Althea wasn't *beautiful,* although she was pleasant-looking. And she was rather meek. Not a girl to be reckoned with," she teased me.

I tried to smile, but I was shaken and too choked to speak. I left a few moments later without reading any poems.

Early one morning after another quarrel with Antipas, Herodias sent for me. "My daughter, I haven't slept a wink. You must prepare yourself for the worst. Hear what your stepfather said to me last night!"

Herodias proceeded to give me a blow-by-blow report of the quarrel, beginning ("In all innocence, Salome!") with her clasping Antipas's hand in both of hers. "I don't want to interfere, my prince," she'd said tenderly, "but I'm afraid the Baptizer's presence is having a demoralizing effect on your people. They say someone in the palace is visiting the dungeon." Her voice rose indignantly. "Someone was even bold enough to send him a basket of food!"

I froze. That someone was Joanna, of course.

Not noticing my reaction, Herodias went on with her story. "So you have an informer among my guards?" Antipas had asked.

"I'm only saying that *you* should have an informer," Herodias had said. "Or perhaps you should have the guards questioned. Or interrogate the preacher himself."

"That would be a bad idea," Antipas had answered. "Torture must be used judiciously. Thank you for your advice, but I already have all the information I need on the Baptizer and his disciples. I know all about the basket of food and its contents. I even know that John gave away the wine to a guard, apparently because he abstains."

Herodias broke off her performance for a moment to comment to me: "Daughter, you can imagine how his cold tone of voice hurt my feelings, when I wish nothing but my husband's welfare. But I did not want to quarrel. I tried not to take offense." She resumed the drama, acting both parts.

"Well!" Herodias had laughed lightly. "My prince's eyes and ears are everywhere!" She went on in a softer tone. "I don't see why you won't send that man to the games master.

A shipment of panthers just arrived at the amphitheater, and the games master says they need more prisoners."

Antipas drew back. "You went to the amphitheater and talked with the games master? What did I tell you about—"

"Oh, never mind all those silly little rules!" Herodias stroked his arm. "Send him to the amphitheater. If you love me, *send the Baptizer to the amphitheater.*"

"Did any of the Jewish leaders see you with the games master?" demanded Antipas.

"The Jewish leaders this, the Jewish leaders that." Herodias gave her musical laugh. "The Jewish leaders have laws against this; they would be offended by that. . . . I begin to wonder who's truly the ruler of Galilee and Perea."

"You know little of ruling," said Antipas to his wife in a distant tone, "if you think a ruler can do whatever he likes. Only twenty years ago, there was a savage uprising in this area. The Romans sent in their troops, and the whole city of Sepphoris was destroyed."

Herodias stepped back and turned away. Over her shoulder, she said, "Perhaps you think you can do whatever you like with *me* and no one will defend me. Know that I have powerful allies among the Herods—and in the Emperor's court."

Antipas had no reply—at least, not in Herodias's telling of the scene.

\* \* \*

That afternoon I went to see Joanna again. "Salome," she said, "you told me how you loved to dance at the Temple of Diana. Would you dance for me today?"

"Oh, yes! I'd like to." I hadn't danced for months. I knew that I missed moving to music, but I hadn't realized how much until just now. "Would you play the music for me?"

Joanna said she had little skill with the lyre, but Zoe could be my musician. I explained to the maid the kind of music I needed. I decided not to dance any of the sacred dances I'd learned at the Temple of Diana, but instead my springtime dance from the performance of *Demeter and Persephone.*

With lemon blossoms tucked into my hair, I danced around Joanna's garden. It wasn't even as large as my father's garden in Rome, and so I kept having to double back on my steps. This threw me a bit off balance, and I stumbled once or twice. But I only laughed, picking up the rhythm again easily. Joanna laughed, too, her face lit up.

"Oh, Salome!" she exclaimed when I'd scattered the last flower. "What a delight! You truly expressed the springtime, fresh and lovely."

While Zoe went to get us a cool drink, I sat down on a stool beside Joanna. Still breathing hard, I rested my head on the edge of the couch. "Your hair is quite wild, my dear!" said

Joanna teasingly. She smoothed the locks from my forehead, and I closed my eyes.

As Joanna stroked my hair, she recited a poem:

> Thou dost show me the path of life;
> in thy presence there is fullness of joy . . .

"That's an old Hebrew poem," murmured Joanna. "But I believe it can be just as true today. It reminds me of John the Baptizer in the Tetrarch's audience hall, how he didn't seem to notice the grandeur of the palace. I think it was because his eyes were on the 'path of life.' "

Alarmed, I opened my eyes. Joanna shouldn't be talking so freely to Herodias's daughter. I blurted, "My mother and stepfather both know that someone sent a basket of food to John the Baptizer."

Joanna stopped smoothing my hair. I sat up, feeling that I'd betrayed my mother. Or was I betraying Joanna by not telling her more?

"Did someone do that?" asked Joanna finally. Her face was closed, as if she'd thrown a veil over it. "How reckless."

# FIFTEEN

# TWO HEROD BROTHERS

Meanwhile, preparations for Antipas's fiftieth birthday celebration were in full swing. He planned a great feast, and he'd invited all the important men in Tiberias as well as those at his court. Some guests would come from as far away as Sepphoris.

The guest of honor would be my uncle Philip, Tetrarch of Gaulanitis, on the other side of Lake Tiberias. I'd seen him years ago when he visited Rome, but I didn't remember him well. Philip was yet another of the Herod half brothers, by yet another wife of my great-grandfather Herod the Great.

During the midday rest a few days before the feast, I went to see Joanna. Visiting Joanna was becoming a habit with me, and I wondered if I might be making a nuisance of my-self. But she always seemed glad to see me.

Today, though, Joanna's maid met me halfway down the path to the steward's house. Joanna wasn't well today, she said. Her mistress hoped to be better tomorrow and to welcome me then.

Disappointed, I wandered back to the palace and into the main garden. On the high wall at one end of the garden, mosaic fish swam in a tile sea. Water poured from a marble dolphin's head into a pool where real fish swam.

I sat on the rim of the pool, watching the flickering shapes. The fish were going busily about their fishy lives, not seem-ing to notice what a cramped little space they were in.

Footsteps, and a shadow fell across the water. I looked up, expecting to see Leander, for he often brought a scroll into the garden to read. Instead, my stepfather's bulky form stood near me on the path. His cold dark eyes were intent on me.

I started up, but Antipas put a hand on my shoulder. "Stay," he said. I sank back, and he sat down beside me. "You looked sad. Were you thinking of Rome? Are you home-sick?" His deep voice was as rich as roast pork. "I think you'll be pleased with the shrine to Diana that I'm building on the market square."

I looked down at my stepfather's robe, right next to my *stola* on the marble seat. It wasn't like him to worry about my feelings. I kept my eyes down as I answered, "I do miss the Temple of Diana and the dancing." I laughed uneasily. "My thoughts just now were silly. I wondered what the fish were thinking."

"Not silly at all—very interesting." His voice grew softer. "Do they worship us? We bring them food, after all. We have the power of life and death over them."

I felt hot and shaky, not exactly with fear, although that was part of it. I had an impulse to jump up and flee, but wouldn't that be rude? Maybe my stepfather was only being friendly. I glanced up at him, then quickly away.

He leaned closer to me, and his breath brushed the side of my face. "Pretty, sleek fish."

The myth of the maiden Europa and the bull—Zeus in disguise—came to my mind. I stood up and took a step back. He also stood up, staring at me. Just as I was about to bolt, he turned and walked out of the garden without another word.

That evening, Herodias and I dined alone. I was uneasy, still agitated by what had happened at the fish pool. Had I behaved immodestly, giving my stepfather the wrong idea? It was not quite proper, for instance, for me to linger in the garden alone during the midday rest.

I was impatient to get back to my room, but Herodias insisted that we take a stroll on the terrace together. Linking her arm in mine, she chatted about this and that. "Doesn't the jasmine smell sweet just after sunset?" She squeezed my arm fondly. "These private moments with my only child mean so much to me."

"The jasmine *is* lovely," I agreed. That seemed safe to say.

"I have a confession to make," Herodias continued with a self-indulgent laugh. "Dear daughter, I admit that I'm a little jealous of your friendship with Joanna. Yes, I know I've devoted a great deal of attention to your stepfather, and perhaps that has caused a distance between you and me."

"Not really," I said. "Well—perhaps a little bit."

"There, you see? And so naturally you have been drawn toward the steward's wife. Salome, I don't like to tell you this . . . but I think you need to know." She paused and turned to clasp both my hands. Her back was to the nearest lamp, and its light shone on my face. "It is strongly suspected, on reliable information, that Joanna has *sent food to the Baptizer*. To our enemy. I am afraid the steward's wife is a follower of the desert preacher."

"I can't believe that!" I muttered.

"I know," sighed Herodias. "She seems so sweet, so mild.

But if you think it over, I believe you'll detect signs of her secret allegiance. For instance, what did she talk to you about this afternoon?"

"I didn't—" I stopped, frightened. If I hadn't visited Joanna this afternoon, what *had* I been doing? "I don't remember. . . ." I turned my face, doubtless covered with guilt, away from the light. "Oh, yes: we read poetry. Joanna recited a Hebrew poem."

"*Mm,* a *Hebrew* poem. The kind of thing the Baptizer spouts." Herodias nodded. "Well, my dear, I know I've revealed something shocking to you. I don't ask you to take it in all at once, and I don't forbid you to visit the steward's wife. But keep your eyes and ears open, and report to me anything that strikes you as suspicious."

"I will, I will." I was relieved that Herodias didn't seem to suspect my stepfather and me. And it should be easy to have nothing much to report about Joanna.

Still, I didn't know what to think or what to do about Antipas's attentions. I longed to confide in someone. The next afternoon, when I visited Joanna, it was on the tip of my tongue the whole time. But I stopped short again and again, afraid of how it would sound. I didn't want Joanna to think badly of me.

Also—I still had the idea that I might use Antipas's interest in me for my own benefit. I was quite sure Joanna wouldn't approve of that. So I said nothing to her about Antipas, and I left the steward's house discontented.

A day or so later, in the morning, I returned from the palace baths by myself. Gundi always went with me, but this time she'd gone back to my room early. I was feeling cheerful, for no reason except a general glow of good health. As I pranced along a colonnade, humming a hymn to Diana, a man stepped out from behind a column.

It was Antipas again. He stood in my way. His expression was almost pleading, as if he needed something badly. He didn't greet me, but began talking in that voice as rich and strong as unwatered wine. "You're as graceful as a nymph today."

"Thank you," I answered.

"My birthday's coming, you know."

"Yes, I know, Stepfather," I said in a strained voice. I backed up against a column, feeling its fluted ridges.

Placing one hand on the column, with the other hand Antipas lifted the amulet hanging from my neck. He examined the charm, resting his hand lightly at the base of my throat. "*Hmm.* The stone is carnelian, isn't it? Pretty, but not pretty enough." His touch seemed to burn, but I stood still as a statue. "I want to give you a costly present on my birthday."

A mixture of fever and alarm roiled my mind, but I had one sharp, clear thought. There *was* something Antipas could give me that I wanted very much. He could forgo the advantages of arranging a political marriage for me; he could send me back to Rome and the Temple of Diana.

But what did he mean by "a costly present"? Something like a pearl necklace? "I couldn't accept it—what would my mother say?"

Antipas trailed one finger across the hollow of my throat, then slowly let the amulet slide down under my tunic. Finally he answered, in a voice almost too low to hear, "Does it matter?"

"I have to go now," I gasped, and I almost ran down the colonnade away from him. Idiot! I scolded myself. I should have asked him right then. Would I get another chance?

Before I reached my room, something else began to worry me. Although I hadn't seen anyone watching Antipas and me, I knew that a servant might have been lurking nearby. They had that knack of being invisible. What if Herodias found out that her husband was . . . *approaching* me?

Gundi, at least, heard about it within a few hours. As she was laying out my clothes for dinner that evening, she chuckled to herself. "So, Cupid's dart has pierced the Tetrarch's chest! Praise to Freya-Aphrodite—we'll have our way yet."

"What are you talking about?" I exclaimed, blushing.

Gundi gave another chuckle, nodding to herself knowingly. "Around the palace, they say that the bull is stalking Europa. *Gundi* says, a clever girl can put a ring in a bull's nose."

"Hold your tongue!" I snapped. My head was pounding, and so was my heart.

As for Herodias, she continued to sulk and quarrel with Antipas. Whenever I saw her, whether it was at lunch, at the baths, or in the garden, she went into long harangues about our family and the special nobility of her father's line. "If only my father, Herod Aristobulus, had lived, none of this would have come to pass!" It was tedious to listen to her; at the same time, it made me nervous. Couldn't she just make up her mind to get along with her husband—the husband she had freely chosen?

Meanwhile, Uncle Philip arrived from across the lake. His brother's grand birthday celebration was still a few days away, but he and Antipas had business to discuss as rulers of neighboring territories. And it seemed that Philip had a third reason for visiting—me.

"This match would be ideal," said Herodias with her winning smile. She was suddenly in a good mood again, maybe looking forward to appearing at the banquet as "Queen" Herodias. "It would cement Antipas's alliance with his brother, and you'd be close enough, in Gaulanitis, to visit here often."

"How can you talk to me like that?" I said. "Doesn't this remind you of the way your delightful first marriage began? And you and Antipas don't even respect Philip as a tetrarch."

"Not every ruler can be an Antipas," said Herodias serenely. "Anyway, when you go to meet Philip, be sure to look your best. Have Gundi curl the locks around your face. And wear your gold bracelet; it's a stunning piece, and it sets off your slender arms." I must have looked blank, because she went on, "You know the bracelet I mean! The double-headed snake."

The gold bracelet that she and Antipas had given me on their wedding day. I'd never told Herodias about losing it, and I'd hoped she'd forgotten it. That was foolish of me. Guiltily, I explained now that I'd dropped the bracelet overboard the first day of our voyage.

"Salome, Salome." Herodias shook her head. "How

could you be so careless?" To my relief, she didn't seem very upset. "Well, wear your matching amber bracelets, then."

Philip sent a note asking me to meet him in the garden off the guest suite so that we could talk in quiet. My heart sank. I couldn't refuse to meet him. Of course I would take Gundi as my chaperone, but her presence might not keep the old goat from *breathing* at me the way my stepfather had.

When I reached the garden, I was surprised to find a younger man than I'd expected. Philip's hair was sprinkled with gray, but he was lean, and his face was boyish. I wasn't even quite sure that this man was my uncle. "Uncle Philip?"

Philip started to say, "Greetings, Salome," but then his jaw dropped and he simply stared at me. It seemed that he was surprised, too. "Salome?"

While Gundi stayed by the garden gate, spinning as usual, Uncle Philip and I sat down near the fountain. We talked about this and that. He asked me if we'd ever been back to the resort on Lake Sabazia, north of Rome.

"There was a shrine there that I liked so much, the way it was set into the hillside with the stream running down the rocks nearby." Philip smiled at me. "As I remember, you put your sandal in the stream to play that it was a boat. You were so surprised when the water carried it away."

I blushed. *I* remembered my mother making fun of me,

and me whining and limping around with one sandal, and finally Uncle Philip carrying me back to the villa.

It seemed that Philip had built a shrine like that near his capital, Caesarea Philippi.

"The whole city is new and clean. Imagine the setting, at the foot of Mount Hermon. From every part of the city, you see the snowcapped peaks. And just outside the walls, I had a park set aside for the people to enjoy. There are meadows, woodland grottos, springs of freshest water. But the shrine is a particularly beautiful place. . . . I'd like you to see it."

His words reminded me uncomfortably of the way Antipas had courted Herodias. Now I was nervous again. Would he nuzzle me? "I'm sure it's lovely," I said. I kept my eyes on the stone path.

"Salome," said Philip quietly, "look at me."

I raised my eyes, expecting to see a hunting stare like the one Antipas had fixed me with. But Philip's eyes were sober and kind.

"Salome," he said, "you must know that an alliance between you and me would be politically advantageous to both the Tetrarch of Galilee and Perea and the Tetrarch of Gaulanitis—me. Maybe you're afraid that my brother and I will put our seals to a marriage contract without consulting your wishes. But my idea is for the two of us to become acquainted with each other and then for both you and me to decide."

I hadn't expected him to be so honest and courteous. I wondered if Philip knew about Antipas's behavior toward me. I stammered something about the honor he did me.

Philip grinned suddenly, looking even younger. "I'll be in Tiberias for several days. We'll talk again."

That afternoon, when I visited Joanna, I told her about my meeting with Philip. "He's a good man," said Joanna, "from what I hear. I'd be glad to see you married to such a ruler." She gave me a fond look. "His wife could have the chance to change his subjects' lives for the better."

"He seemed kind," I said uncomfortably. Joanna had a vision of my future, and it didn't fit at all with my own vision: to get my stepfather to send me back to the Temple of Diana. Herodias—I shut my mind to that problem. If I ignored her wishes and appealed to Antipas, she'd be fit to bite the head off a marble statue.

The next morning, Philip asked me to walk with him on the upper terrace. As we leaned on the balustrade, he pointed across Lake Tiberias to the bluffs on the eastern shore. "My tetrarchy may not be as rich in fertile soil as Galilee, but the air is fresh and clean there, in the highlands."

"I suppose I've gotten used to the air in Tiberias," I said. "When I first arrived, it seemed like the steam room at the baths."

"I wouldn't like to get used to this climate," said Philip. A grim note in his voice disturbed me—did he disapprove of me for getting used to it? Or was he hinting at something else?

Philip went on to tell me about Gaulanitis and his other territories. "The people are a mixed lot," he said. "In the cities, the people are mainly Greeks and Romans; in the countryside, mainly Syrians; and in the eastern parts, tribes of Arab nomads. When I first inherited the tetrarchy, years ago, I thought of course I'd govern from my capital city. But I became curious about how my people lived, and so I picked up the habit of traveling among them and talking to them in their own town squares." He smiled. "What a difference from sitting in my grand audience hall (not that it's nearly as magnificent as Antipas's hall) and letting my subjects approach my throne! They spoke much more freely to me."

I thought of John the Baptizer. Antipas's magnificent hall hadn't stopped *him* from speaking freely. I was going to ask Philip if he'd heard about John, but Philip continued.

"Forgive me for droning on about my ideas of statecraft. I assure you that not many rulers would agree with me, least of all my half brother here!" He laughed ruefully. "The point I meant to make is that I spend much of the year traveling around my territories. Of course my wife could stay home in comfort in the capital, Caesarea Philippi." He glanced sideways at me. "Or she could travel with me if . . ."

I looked at him in surprise. Now he sounded shy—almost wistful. I had an impulse to reach up and ruffle his short gray-sprinkled hair. I hoped Philip wouldn't be very angry when he found out he'd wasted time courting me.

"Well!" said Philip in a businesslike tone. "It's something to think about. Meanwhile, Antipas expects me to join him for a tour of his building projects in Tiberias. Until later, Salome." With a polite bow, he strode past Gundi and disappeared through the flowering shrubs.

I'd missed my chance to tell him that traveling around would suit me much better than sitting in a palace. But what difference did it make? I wouldn't do either if I had my way—if I escaped to Rome and the Temple of Diana.

# SIXTEEN

# THE TETRARCH REPENTS

The palace kitchens were right above the prison, and the aromas of simmering sauces, baking pastries, and roasting meats drifted down to the cells. "They're cooking for the Tetrarch's banquet, three days away," the jailer told John.

John didn't ask what the menu was, but the jailer told him anyway. "There'll be fish from Lake Tiberias, fricasseed in white wine, leeks, and oregano. There'll be lamb stewed with onions, cumin, and pepper. There'll be whole pigeons in fig syrup. Any dish you can think of and a lot you couldn't—but no pork." The jailer snickered, looked over his shoulder to make sure no one was listening, and added, "Prince

Antipas respects the Jewish dietary laws, you know." He laughed again.

On the night before the banquet, two visitors came to John's cell. The first, early in the evening, was the Tetrarch's Greek secretary. John remembered seeing him in the audience hall by Antipas's throne.

"Teacher, I know you're a good man," the young man whispered through the bars of the cell. "And I want to live a good life. But how can I? I swore to my dying father that I'd provide dowries for my sisters. If I leave the Tetrarch, my sisters will have nothing, and then who would marry them? But to get the money, I'm serving an evil master. You see my dilemma?"

John was touched by the Greek, who seemed as sincere as any of the people who came to the banks of the Jordan. John could well imagine how demoralizing it would be to live at the Tetrarch's elbow, recording his heartless acts and his appalling thoughts.

"Tell me, what should I do?" Leander gripped the bars as if he were the prisoner. "Which is a higher duty: duty to my family or duty to the Truth? I know it's right to keep my promise to my dying father."

John nodded. "As the Law says, Honor your father and your mother."

"But if keeping my promise causes me to do wrong," pleaded the Greek secretary, "may I be released from the promise?"

John shook his head. But he felt sorry for Leander, even though he was a Gentile. Reaching through the bars, he put a hand on the Greek's head and blessed him. He said a prayer of King David's: "Deliver me, O Lord, from evil men . . ."

Not long after Leander left, Antipas reappeared. This time, he had a goblet in his hand. A cupbearer, a young boy, stood behind the Tetrarch with a pitcher.

"I want you to know I've been taking your words to heart," Antipas told John. "As I mentioned, it's my fiftieth birthday tomorrow—time to reflect and consider." He held the goblet out to his side, and the boy refilled it. "Yes, Baptizer, you're right. I've been remiss about following Jewish law. It's time I took my position as ruler of the Jews more seriously. Tomorrow night, I intend to set an example for the important men of Galilee. So I've had all the statues in the great hall removed and put away in the storerooms. The wall paintings were more of a problem, but then I hit upon the idea of hanging draperies to cover them.

"And the mosaic on the floor in the front atrium—I don't suppose you'd have seen that, Baptizer. The guards would have brought you in through the barracks courtyard. Anyway, it's a mosaic of Pan playing his pipes for dancing nymphs. It cost me a pile of gold, as you can imagine, but never mind!— I'm covering it up. The butler found a large rug with a geometric pattern to hide the mosaic."

John said, "Why does Herod Antipas come down to the prison to tell me about his statues and rugs?"

"It all has to do with repenting and following the Jewish Law," said Antipas patiently. "I said to myself, if I am called to lead the Jewish people to their glory, I ought to be a little more observant of the Law of Moses." He stroked his beard thoughtfully. "I may even give up pork for private meals."

Was the man drunk? Out of his mind? The Tetrarch seemed to hint that he was . . . John connected this hint with Antipas's talk of prophecies, and his mind staggered. Antipas must be possessed by Satan to think such blasphemy.

Draining his goblet, Antipas held it out again for the boy to refill. "I see you're surprised," he remarked to John. "You thought I'd been angered by your harsh words the other day. Yes, at first I was, but later I began to see the sense in them." He leaned forward and lowered his voice, as if to confide something important. "I've been wondering—I've actually been wondering if I was too hasty in marrying Herodias."

"In the eyes of the Lord, you did *not* marry Herodias." John didn't expect Antipas to listen, but he would speak the truth anyway. "She is still your brother's wife, and the Nabatean woman whom you put aside for no good reason is still your wife."

"If I made the wrong decision there," said Antipas, "I've already been punished for it. That woman's moods! Her nagging!" He rolled his eyes. "In Rome, when she was still my brother's wife, she was nothing but charm. Almost like a goddess. She'd say things to me like, 'We two, of all the family, are the true heirs of Herod the Great. Who knows how high we can climb?' " He gave a short laugh. "She must have had me under a spell. Risking war with Nabatea! Making an enemy of my brother!"

The Tetrarch folded his arms and nodded, as if he'd come to a weighty decision. "There will be no women among my guests tonight." Raising his goblet in a salute to John, he drained it once more. "We'll talk of this again, Baptizer. I'll need a prophet in my court."

# SEVENTEEN

# THE BIRTHDAY GIFT

On the morning of Antipas's birthday dinner, I was glad to run into Leander outside the library. "Is that more of the Tetrarch's diary?" I asked, pointing to the sheaf of parchment under his arm.

"Yes." Leander looked over his shoulder, as if someone might be listening to us. "It's all about how he's following the Jewish Law now." He shook his head. "When I think of the Jewish philosophers I knew in Alexandria and how they loved and honored their Law . . . Whereas Antipas's idea of devotion to the highest principles is, he's not going to serve pork at the banquet." Leander laughed sardonically. "That reminds me of a joke. . . ."

"What joke?" I naturally asked. Leander seemed to have second thoughts about sharing the joke with me, but I begged him. I could see he was itching to tell it, against his better judgment.

"Well, then," he said. "This is something the Emperor Caesar Augustus said years ago about his friend Herod the Great. You know that King Herod had killed three of his own sons? At the same time, he thought he was being a virtuous Jew because he wouldn't eat pork! So when the Emperor heard this, he said, 'I'd rather be Herod's pig than his son.' "

We both laughed. But while I was still giggling, Leander's expression turned worried. "I meant no disrespect to your great-grandfather, Miss Salome, or to any of your family, of course."

This struck me as even funnier, and I laughed again. "*Of course* you did mean disrespect—that's why it was funny."

Leander looked at the floor and spoke in a constricted voice. "I should not have repeated that story. People who displease the Tetrarch end up in a dungeon, like John the Baptizer. Or as fish food, like that fool Simon."

"I would never betray a friend," I said with a rush of feeling. Then I blushed. I was forgetting that after all, Leander was only a secretary. It wasn't proper for me to address him as a friend. To change the subject, I asked about his mother and sisters.

Leander had sent more money to his mother yesterday, he said, to start a dowry for his second sister. "I'm keeping my eyes on the goal," he remarked. "After I've earned enough to settle my sisters, I'll be free to leave for Alexandria." He smiled one of his rare smiles. "Perhaps a year from now, my time of service to the Tetrarch will be only an entertaining story to tell the other students at Demo's school."

It made me sad to see how eager Leander was to get away from this place. Of course, I was, too—but I would miss *him*. And I was rather hurt that he'd mistrusted me about the pork joke. I nodded politely and walked away.

Later that morning, I started for the baths. In the great hall, at the bottom of the steps, I passed Herodias. That is, I started to pass her, but the fury on her face stopped me cold. "Why—what's the matter?"

Herodias's eyes flicked around the hall, as if looking for spies. I'd never seen her so distraught. Her lips quivered as she said, "He's thinking of putting me aside. To please the Jews."

I started to protest, but she went on, "*I* know what's on his mind. First he had the statues taken out of sight and the wall paintings covered up. I said to him, 'Really, if the Jews wish to join the modern world . . .'

"And he interrupted me—rather rudely—and he said, 'I realize you've spent most of your life in Rome, but still you should understand that the Jews do *not* wish to join the modern world. I've explained to you more than once, I don't want to appear to slight their customs. For that reason, I don't invite wives to state dinners such as this.' "

Herodias paused for breath, scowling. "I said, 'In Rome, no one of importance would give a birthday feast without inviting wives.' And he said, 'We are not in Rome.'

" 'Indeed,' I replied. 'Are you considering *me* at all? Who shall I talk with, then? I'm not interested in discussing men's business all evening.'

"And Antipas said—with such a brutal note in his voice, staring at me with his piggy little eyes—'That won't be necessary.' Yes—he talked to me like that, in front of his butler and his prissy Greek secretary! He said, 'The Jewish leaders would be offended if I included any women at this public event. They're very sensitive to slights.'

"I thought, I, too, am sensitive to slights, but I didn't say that out loud. I said, 'Perhaps the prince ought to invite that filthy desert man to preach to his guests about the Law of Moses. That should please the Jews.'

"And do you know what he said then?" Herodias's mouth trembled with outrage. "He told me to be silent. Me, granddaughter of Herod the Great! He said, 'Go to your rooms, woman . . . and think about the Nabatean princess who *used* to live in those rooms.' "

I fumbled to come up with a soothing response, but Herodias was not listening to me. A strange expression came over her face, as if she'd had a sudden thought. "Wait!" she exclaimed to herself. "What was under that *other* hanging?" Whirling, she rushed back into the great hall.

I went on to the bathhouse, troubled. Herodias was not only furious—she was terrified. Perhaps Antipas really was thinking of divorcing her.

I undressed and sat down on a bench in the *tepidarium*, the warm room. As Gundi cleaned my back with oil and a scraper, I gazed across the hall at a statue of Hera, queen of the gods. She was as beautiful as Aphrodite, but in a soft, motherly way.

As I mused, a woman appeared in the doorway at the end of the long room. Through the steamy air of the baths, I didn't realize at first that it was Herodias again. She looked like some kind of avenging spirit, her form taut with anger. Then I saw it was my mother, and I braced myself to hear her rant on about what else Antipas had done.

Herodias stalked right up to me, staring like a lioness fixing her prey. "You deceitful . . . little . . . slut." She stressed each word by slapping my face, right-left-right. I thought she'd gone mad.

Before I could even protest, Herodias went on, "I just had a look at Antipas's fine new painting. He'd covered it with a drape, like all the others, but I *thought* there hadn't been a painting there before." She mimed lifting a drape. "And what do you suppose? A nymph, her hair floating loose around her, wearing a crown of ivy and very little else, being chased by a satyr." She made a scornful gesture at me. I pulled a towel around myself.

"The paint was fresh," said Herodias in a meaningful tone, "not more than a few days old. The picture showed just a hint of fear in her eyes—what a tastefully erotic touch." Herodias leaned toward me with a frightening smile. "And *who* do you suppose the nymph was?"

I was afraid I knew, but I shook my head.

"Liar! How could you think of such treachery to your own mother?"

"No—I didn't know about—" I stammered. I stood up, clutching the towel to me. "He came to *me*—he wanted me to—"

"So you thought to become a tetrarch's wife." Herodias laughed unpleasantly. "Not the tetrarch of Gaulanitis, either."

"No, please, Herodias!" A lock of my hair fell out of the

clasp, and I twisted it desperately. "I swear by Diana, I never—"

Herodias turned on Gundi, standing by with the pitcher of scented oil and the scraper. "As for *you*—how could you let this happen? You had only one simple job, to chaperone Salome. You ungrateful old hag. The next market day, I'll send you to the slave dealer. Maybe someone will want an ugly woman to scrub floors in a brothel."

Whipping back to me, Herodias raged on: "Apparently it *is* high time for you to be married so that you don't wander around like a heifer in rut. Antipas was right in the first place: he should give you to the prince of Nabatea." She gave her musical laugh. "That's where you belong, with that dirty princess."

Then Herodias stalked off. I looked at Gundi and burst into tears. But Gundi said, "Never mind, little one. We shall see—we shall see." Leading me to the warm pool, she splashed water over my shoulders with the dipper. Her face was hard and set, an expression I had never seen on Gundi before.

After a swim in the cold pool, I felt calmer. I came out into the exercise yard of the baths thinking that I'd go to my mother's suite. She'd be calmer, too, and probably regretting her wild words.

Besides, there was really no reason to be afraid of my mother. Here in Galilee, Antipas was the supreme power. He seemed to like me—and why should he do anything Herodias advised? According to her, he was on the point of putting her aside.

On the grassy field the entertainers for the banquet—jugglers, acrobats, musicians, and dancers—were practicing. I paused to watch them. Antipas was already watching from the other side of the field, outside the men's entrance to the baths. I didn't expect him to approach me in this public place, but almost as soon as he saw me, he walked across the yard.

"Little Salome, I'm glad you have this chance to see the entertainers for the feast. My butler found some good ones, don't you think?"

I nodded, thinking only of what I wanted him to do for me. "My lord stepfather, I would ask—"

Not waiting to hear my request, he went on in a soft voice, "Believe me, I wish with all my heart that women—especially one young woman—could be included in the banquet tonight."

I was confused. Did he think I was going to ask to come to the banquet?

"Please understand," Antipas went on, "it's a political matter. Don't take it personally. Tomorrow night we'll have another fine celebration, just my court, with statues, paint-ings, *and* women—even pork!"

Then, although Gundi was standing next to me, he leaned close and murmured, "But tonight, I hope a certain beautiful girl will give Antipas a special birthday gift."

I trembled inside, but I said boldly, "I thought my lord was going to give that girl a special gift." I didn't look at him, but kept my eyes on the dancer going through her routine.

"Indeed he is." My stepfather, too, looked straight ahead. The dancer twirled across the exercise yard, throwing off layer after layer of gauzy scarves. "He wishes to exchange gifts with her on his birthday. Do you know what he longs for above all things?"

I shook my head.

"He wants her to . . . *dance* for him."

"At the banquet?" I was so shocked that I turned to stare at him. I hadn't expected him to suggest something so inde-cent, for a girl of good family to dance in public.

"Of course not." Antipas kept his expression bland, but his breathing was heavy. "In private."

# EIGHTEEN

# THE SCORPION STRIKES

After Antipas left, Gundi began to speak in a hard voice to match her new expression. She had a plan, a well-thought-out plan. It must have been simmering in her mind for some time.

The moment had come, Gundi said. "Don't you see what's happening? Your mother's heading for a fall. The Tetrarch's leading up to putting her aside. Her boat is sinking. If you leap boldly, you can leave that little boat and land in the royal barge."

What Gundi meant was that if Antipas did put Herodias aside, naturally I would have to leave the palace, too. Unless I was the new wife. Gundi had thought of a way I could ask Antipas at a moment when he couldn't say no.

I put my hands over my ears to shut out Gundi's voice. I didn't want to "land in the royal barge." I wanted to escape to Rome and a safe life in the Temple of Diana.

Back in the palace, I ordered Gundi to stay in my room while I went to Herodias's suite. Surely my mother would be calm enough to listen to reason now. I'd explain that I only wanted to return to the Temple of Diana and serve the goddess. Herodias would have nothing to fear from Antipas's interest in me if she helped me get back to Rome.

But when I reached Herodias's suite, the double doors were bolted from the inside. Iris nervously informed me, without opening the doors, that Lady Herodias was resting. Unheeding, I tapped and called my mother's name over and over.

When I had almost given up, I was startled by a scream through the closed door. "Iris! Tell that girl I know exactly what she's up to!"

The words "that girl" chilled me—I'd never heard her talk about me like that. Still, I thought "what she's up to" meant what Herodias had said before, that I intended to become Antipas's new wife. I tried to explain that what I really wanted was to get back to Rome and the Temple of Diana. But her piercing voice cut through my words. "That girl, a servant of the chaste Diana? What an amusing idea."

My heart sank. Instead of calming down, Herodias had worked herself into an insane frenzy. I had never heard her like this. "No, wait—listen—"

"It all fits together," Herodias went on in a cold voice that frightened me more than her screams. "Oh, it's clear as crystal now. She's in a plot with the steward's wife. That's why she wouldn't talk about her little trysts with that woman. And that's where the gold bracelet went—to bribe the prison guards, to help the Baptizer."

Herodias went on and on. She'd worked out all the details of my "plot," with my every action imagined as part of it. "Well, I can plot, too," she finished in a deadly whisper. "There are many ways to deal with an enemy."

"No, Herodias! I would never . . ." My voice trailed away helplessly. Herodias was unhinged. I was afraid of her. Of course, she might be sorry later. Herodias might even cry, the way King Herod the Great had cried over the sons he'd executed by mistake.

This was what it meant to be a Herod—to trust no one. Pushing myself away from the doors, I walked slowly back to my room.

"Gundi," I said, "that was a good idea you had." I wouldn't wait like a helpless calf for someone else to decide my fate. I was a Herod, so why not act like a Herod and make my own fate? Not the one that Herodias, Antipas, or even Gundi wanted.

Gundi and I went over the details of our plan. She'd already taken it upon herself to speak to the dancer and suggest a bargain: I'd borrow the dancer's costume and her role for the banquet. She'd take the evening off with twice the pay.

As we were planning, Joanna's maid, Zoe, appeared with a message. Joanna was feeling better than usual. She was especially eager to see me today, because she'd decided to ask me something.

Gundi made shooing motions at the other maid. "Miss Salome is very busy this afternoon."

In fact, I was just about to return to the exercise field to meet the dancer and practice with the scarves. "Tell your mistress I'll visit her tomorrow," I said to Zoe. I felt a pang of regret. At the back of my mind a thought hovered briefly: After tomorrow, nothing will be the same.

But I must not lose my nerve. They say that when a gladiator is sent from the holding pens under the amphitheater into the arena, they bolt the gates behind him. The gladiator can't choose to return to the pens to avoid the battle. He's in the arena. If he wants to live, he has to fight. Now I knew how the gladiators felt.

By the end of my practice session with the dancer, the sun was low in the sky. I hurried back from the exercise field, for the banquet was about to begin.

The servants, all those not needed for the moment, were watching from the balcony overlooking the great dining hall. I paused to watch with them, for it was as good as going to the theater. As each splendidly dressed guest arrived, he was crowned with a wreath and announced by the master of the feast, then escorted down the length of the hall to Prince Antipas.

At Antipas's couch the guest would bow—low or not so low, depending on his rank. The Tetrarch greeted him and presented him with a gift. Then Chuza led the guest to his place on the proper couch—near Antipas's head table or not so near, depending again on the guest's rank.

Uncle Philip, the guest of honor, reclined on a couch next to Antipas. I thought he looked uncomfortable in his stiff embroidered robes. He mopped sweat from his brow with a napkin.

I couldn't hear what the two Tetrarchs were saying, but their actions were like a little mime show, the meaning clear without words. Antipas beckoned his cupbearer to pour more wine. Philip put his hand over his goblet. Antipas drained his own goblet, and the cupbearer refilled it. Philip gave his half brother a sideways glance, as though he'd endured many such evenings with Antipas.

As the servers below carried in the quails' eggs and olives, the dancer tapped my shoulder. "We'd better go to your room, Miss Salome. It'll take longer than you think to get you made up."

Gundi was waiting in my bedchamber, looking satisfied. "I took a peek at her. Must have already drunk her evening wine—sleeping like a pig." I knew Gundi meant Herodias, although she had not said "my lady."

The dancer motioned me to sit on the bed. Setting out pots and jars of cosmetics, brushes, combs, and pins, she got to work on my face like a painter on a statue. "You've got large eyes with long lashes," she said approvingly as she lined my eyelids with kohl. "The eyes must stand out, because the lower half of your face will be covered with the veil for most of the dance."

While the dancer stroked on paints and powders, she chatted happily. She was delighted she was going home early this evening, before her children were asleep. Her little girl always asked, "Mama, will you stay home tonight? Mama, will you kiss me good night before I go to sleep?" The dancer gave a wistful laugh. "I have to tell her no, Mama has to dance for money again so that my darling will have bread to eat tomorrow."

Meanwhile, Gundi was busy with her statuette in a corner. I couldn't turn my head to see what she was doing, but I smelled incense. "What are you up to, Gundi?" She didn't answer, but I heard her speak the name of Freya-Aphrodite.

The dancer painted my fingernails with a rosy stain. Opening a jar of musky perfume, she touched my wrists and neck. "This scent fills the air as you dance. It drives them mad," she added with a wink.

Next, the dancer brought out a gilt loincloth and brassiere. "This costume is a copy from a statue of Aphrodite in Pompeii," she said proudly as she helped me put on the scanty undergarments. "The finest workmanship." She hung showy gilt earrings from my ears and pushed bracelets and anklets on my arms and legs.

Then she draped and pinned the scarves around me, beginning with a veil for my lower face. One last time, I practiced shedding the scarves smoothly as part of the dance. I had it perfectly—it was an easy routine, really, more like a series of poses than a dance.

But as the dancer was leaving, bowing and smiling and vowing to name her next daughter after me, I lost my nerve. "Wait! I can't do this." I pulled off the face veil. "I'm sorry about your little girl. I'll pay you even more—but I can't do this." My knees trembled, and my stomach quivered, worse than aboard ship. Running to the slops jar, I was sick.

Behind me I heard murmurs: worried questions from the dancer, firm answers from Gundi. Then Gundi knelt beside me, holding my head. She wiped my face. "There, there. No harm done. Nothing got on the scarves."

I still felt shaky, but relieved. Now, I thought, Gundi must understand that I couldn't possibly go down to the banquet hall and dance in front of all those men and demand a reward from my stepfather.

Putting some dried herbs on the brazier, Gundi had me breathe in the smoke. I began to feel better—much better—almost carefree. I noticed that the dancer was no longer in the room, and I assumed she'd gone downstairs to start her dance. But she'd left her costume with me. Maybe she had another one?

The dancer had left her paints and brushes, too, because Gundi was touching up my lips again, murmuring, "There we go, good as new."

I didn't understand why Gundi was fastening the last veil over my face again, pulling me toward the door. I knew I wasn't going to dance, but I went along to please her. It didn't worry me that she was so mistaken—in fact, it was funny. "Gundi, you old silly . . ."

Outside my room, I felt everything around me almost as if it had become part of me: the smooth tile under my feet, the soft air flowing along the corridor, the scarves lightly brushing my arms and legs. My hips swayed as I walked. Passing a panel of polished black marble, I glimpsed a vision deep in the stone.

It was the goddess of love, with wispy garments and glittering ornaments adorning her divine beauty. Her smooth shoulders and arms gleamed through the gaps in her gauzy clothing. Her eyes were accented with kohl, her full mouth stained red. "Gundi," I said wonderingly. "You've called up Aphrodite."

"Yes, and she's with you," whispered Gundi. "Go." Pulling me gently to the top of the stairs, she let go of my hand.

Down in the banquet hall, the dinner was coming to an end. Servers carried in trays of fruit and sweetmeats, while other slaves lit the lamps. I descended the stairs with deliberate steps, scarves trailing. Under the flimsy costume, I felt my body glowing like hot gold.

Antipas, in spite of all the wine he'd drunk, noticed me

coming down the stairs. "Aha!" he called out. A gong
was struck, and the hubbub of conversation in the hall died
away. "Think you'll enjoy this," he announced to his guests.
"Picked her out myself. Dances with real feeling." As I'd
planned, he thought I was the dancer he'd hired.

The musicians were waiting for my signal. I nodded.
Drumming began, growing slowly louder as I stepped into a
shaft of sunset light, and the guests turned their heads toward
me. "Ahh," I heard them breathe. Antipas watched with a
pleased expression, his eyes half closed.

I lifted my arms to begin the dance, and the musicians
started a slow melody on the pipes. A light drumbeat pulsed
underneath.

I wove my way around the dining couches. I didn't look
directly at any of the men, but from the corner of my eye, I
saw them staring at me. I let the first scarf float to the floor,
and the cymbals sent a shiver of sound through the hall. I was
borne along on the dance the way I used to be, dancing for
Diana.

But now I serve another goddess, I thought. Aphrodite.
Her power is mine. I feel it trailing out behind me, filling the
hall, like the scent of my perfume.

Another scarf unwound and floated away from my body.
The cymbals rang. One man lifted the scarf from the floor

without taking his eyes off me and pressed the cloth to his mouth. I danced on and on, shedding the lengths of gauze one after the other, until the steps brought me before Antipas's couch.

In a sweeping motion I pulled the veil off my face and the clasp from my hair. Sliding to the floor, I bent backward so that my body arched from my toes to my fingers, with my loosened hair brushing the tiles. With a last throb of the drum, the music ceased.

The hall was still, except for the sound of men breathing. I rose to my knees. One of the musicians had gathered up the scarves, and she now wrapped them around me. But my face was bare. "Here is my gift for your birthday, O prince," I said.

Antipas licked his lips. "A priceless gift," he answered in a hoarse voice.

"I await my reward." My voice sounded shrill in the hall full of important men. Inside my head, Aphrodite seemed to laugh in delight at my boldness. Philip, on the couch next to Antipas, stared at me. At the edge of my thoughts, I wished he weren't here to see me act like—like a Herod. But I couldn't think about that now. I spoke again, louder. "The prince promised a generous gift."

Around me the guests grinned and beat their goblets on

the tables. "Yes! Reward the dancer!" Most of them had no idea who I was.

"By the gods, you shall have your reward." Antipas stretched a hand across the table toward me, the sleeve of his robe brushing the sweetmeats on a silver platter. He cleared his throat, and his voice became stronger. "Whatever you wish." Applause echoed through the hall, then died away as the guests leaned forward to hear my request.

"Whatever I wish?" I said breathlessly. The moment had come.

"Whatever you wish. Do you want gold, pearls, all the treasure in my storerooms?" At Antipas's last reckless suggestion, I saw Steward Chuza half rise from his couch, wringing his hands. Antipas paid no attention. "If you wish it, I will give you . . . *half my kingdom.*" His eyes locked mine, and he added in a whisper, "You know what I mean."

I did know. He meant exactly what Gundi had intended. But it wasn't what I intended.

Antipas went on, loud enough for all to hear, "I, Herod Antipas, son of Herod the Great, swear it on my honor as Tetrarch of Galilee and Perea. If you wish it, I will give you half my kingdom."

Now I would say, "Send me back to Rome, to the Temple

of Diana." If only I had spoken without looking around! But I heard a sound—a moan—from the direction of the stairs. I did look around.

A woman stood on the bottom step, clutching the pedestal of the lamp stand. For a moment I thought it was Herodias. But wasn't Herodias upstairs, deep in a drugged sleep? Besides, this woman looked older.

"Daughter!"

It *was* Herodias. Only, this was the Herodias I had glimpsed during my night in the Temple of Diana—a small, weak person. It hurt me to see her like this, stripped of her beauty and charm, surrounded by enemies. Yes, Antipas had filled his grand hall with Herodias's enemies, men who wished her ill. Most of them would be glad to see Herodias put aside by Antipas and turned out of the palace.

My mother was now hastening across the dining hall, around clusters of couches and tables, toward me. There was terror, and a desperate hope, on her face. Pity wrung my heart.

No pity, however, showed in Antipas's stare at his wife. "I thought I made it clear that women were not to come to this banquet."

Chuza leaned toward him. "Shall I call the guards, my lord?"

"No!" I cried out, not pleading but commanding. "Leave her alone."

My stepfather swung his head around to regard me. His eyelids were half closed, and he spoke slowly. "You get only one wish. Choose carefully."

Flinging herself onto the floor in front of me, Herodias clutched my ankles. She kissed my feet. "I pray you, dearest, kindest daughter, let me stay with you. Oh, protect me. I beg of you!"

My mother and I should not be enemies. It was Antipas, and all such powerful men, who turned us women against each other, like gladiators who should have been friends.

Herodias raised her head, her eyelashes sparkling with tears. From my towering height of divine strength, I was glad to offer my protection to this poor woman. I bent down and pulled her up.

"Oh, child of my heart," whispered Herodias. "If only you will claim the courage and wisdom of our royal ancestors, you can save us both! It all depends on what you ask for."

"What shall I ask?" I whispered back.

Squeezing my hand, Herodias told me what she wanted.

I felt a shock of horror, but then understanding sank into me. I saw through Aphrodite's eyes, free of the human notions of right and wrong. If I forced Antipas to do what

Herodias wanted, no one could touch her. He'd be casting his lot with his wife, against the Jews who wanted her put aside.

Now Herodias and I were as close as I could have wished when I was a little girl. Only, this was not the cozy closeness of my childhood. It was a closeness shaped by the sad, bleak truth: the world was against us. Our charmed circle was the circle formed by two gladiators swinging their swords.

I took a deep breath. "I wish the head of John, called the Baptizer!" My voice rang from the lavishly decorated ceiling. "As you swore on your honor, O prince."

# NINETEEN

# THE VALLEY OF THE
# SHADOW OF DEATH

In his prison cell under the banquet hall, John heard footsteps coming down the corridor. He recognized that tread: it was the evening-shift jailer. The door was unbarred and opened a crack. "Baptizer, your disciple left a message." The man handed over a tablet and held up his torch so that John could read it.

*To Rabbi John the Baptizer from Elias his disciple,* began the note scratched in the wax surface of the tablet. *I hoped to see you in person to tell you about Rabbi Yeshua. We found him still in Nain, where we heard him preach. Rabbi, we were filled with joy. Your cousin said, Repent, the kingdom of the Lord is at hand. And afterward he healed many who were sick, blind, and tormented by demons. Then I asked him your question, if he was the One Who Is to Come. He answered, Tell John what you have seen and heard today.*

John sighed deeply. "Thanks be to the Lord."

The jailer cleared his throat. "Baptizer . . . your disciple had no money to pay me for giving you the message. He said you would bless me instead."

Lifting his gaze from the tablet, John saw a strange expression on the jailer's face. "I'm not a magician, jailer," he said. "I could say a blessing over you, but it would mean nothing unless you repented."

The jailer was silent for a moment. Then, keeping his eyes fixed on John's face, he sank to his knees. "What should I do to repent, Rabbi?"

Even here, Lord! thought John. Even in the depths of the Tetrarch's prison, the Lord's call was heard. "Be merciful to the prisoners you guard," he told the man. "Give them their bread and water, let them have visitors without taking bribes. And when you have lived this way for a month . . ."

John hesitated. At this point in instructing the penitent, he always told them to return to him to be baptized. But now he knew, with a feeling as solid as these stone walls, that he would never baptize again. "When you have lived this way for a month, go find Rabbi Yeshua of Nazareth."

A little later, John heard footsteps coming down the corridor toward his cell. There were two pairs of feet this time, and one of them wore heavy-soled soldier's sandals. While the jailer's footsteps had been cautious, almost sneaky, these footsteps slapped the stone floor with thoughtless force. A man who walked this way had no qualms about his assignment, no secret desire for blessing.

John felt the presence, invisible but solid, of the prophet Elijah. And Amos, Ezekiel, Isaiah . . . all the prophets gone before John gathered now to lend him strength. Peace, John, they said.

A line of torchlight appeared under the cell door, and the footsteps stopped. The iron bar on the door clanked as someone fumbled with it. "Hurry up, you," said the soldier. "They're waiting upstairs." There was a rasp of steel—the unsheathing of a sword.

John prayed his last prayer, a prayer of King David. *"Though I walk through the valley of the shadow of death, I will fear no evil, for Thou art with me."*

# TWENTY

# TRAGEDY

The Tetrarch gave the order, and a guard left with the silver platter for the prison. The great hall was silent. Time passed. It almost seemed that I could hear the drip of the water clock all the way from the entrance hall. Antipas did not move. He looked stunned, like a wrestler thrown to the ground by a man half his size.

I was stunned, too. What had happened? Aphrodite had left me. I was no longer a goddess—I was just a young girl without a protector. I felt sick and weak. Be strong, I told myself. Remember your ancestors Lady Salome and Queen Alexandra.

Here comes the guard with the platter. On the platter, a

thing with a face. Eyes and mouth open, chalky gray skin. Like a theater mask for tragedy. Do not look closely at it. Steeling myself, I held out my hands.

"Woe! Accursed day!" As Antipas cried out, I nearly dropped the heavy platter.

Seizing his gold-embroidered robe with both hands, Antipas ripped it down the front. Then he walked out of the hall. Philip followed him, then their attendants, and then the rest of the guests. Some of the men cast horrified glances at me; others stared straight ahead.

I was left standing before Antipas's couch by myself, holding the platter. I managed not to look directly at it, but I couldn't help feeling the weight. I gripped the handles so tightly that the edges of the silver grape leaves cut into my hands. I turned my eyes aside to the empty wine goblets on the table. I smelled blood, and I tried not to breathe very much.

A thought came into my numb mind: Herodias, it was Herodias who had asked for this. I would give it to her. I turned toward my mother.

In a firm, kind voice, as though I were six years old, she said, "Salome, set that down on the table. Here, I'll clear a place." She moved the goblets to one side.

Carefully, as if I were serving a choice dish to invisible guests, I stooped to set the platter down on Antipas's table.

"Good girl." Herodias put an arm around my shoulders. "Now come with me." She led me across the hall. In the lamplight her face glowed.

As we climbed the stairs together, she kissed my hair, whispered in my ear. "You did so well, my dearest dear! What a brave girl."

"Oh, Mama!" I gasped.

Near the top of the stairs I glanced up at the balcony. The audience of servants had melted away, all except Leander and Gundi. Leander stared as if I were the Medusa and he were turned to stone at the sight. Then he wrenched his gaze away, and he, too, disappeared. Gundi, leaning on the balcony railing, did not turn away, but her expression was bleak.

"Gundi," said Herodias. "Go to my suite and fetch the pitcher and cup from my bedside table. Bring them to Salome's room." She guided me along the loggia.

In my room we sat on the couch until Gundi brought the pitcher. Herodias gave me sips from her own delicate glass cup. The wine was sweet with honey, covering up a bitter taste. "Now the danger is past," murmured Herodias. "Now we can breathe freely."

"It looked like a mask," I choked out. "A mask from a tragedy—do you know what I mean?"

"Of course Antipas was upset," Herodias went on, "but

he'll come around. He'll realize that he should have taken care of it himself some time ago. He'll convince himself that it was all his own idea."

Gradually my distress faded, soothed away by the drug in the wine and Herodias's murmurs. "There, there. The worst is over now." Her voice stroked me while her hand rubbed the back of my neck.

When I was calmer, Herodias had Gundi help me out of the dancer's costume. Leading me to my bed, Herodias tucked a warm robe around me. The last thing I heard before I sank into a stupor was, "Sleep well, my dearest pet."

# TWENTY-ONE

# MURDERER

I woke up late, knowing before I was really awake that I wanted to stay asleep. Then I remembered why. My mind shied aside, the way my gaze had shied from the platter last night.

But sunlight filtered through the lattice doors. Could the worst be over, as Herodias had said? I tried to talk to Gundi as she brought water for me to wash my face and offered bread and figs. I wasn't hungry, and her grim silence didn't help my appetite.

Then Herodias appeared, smiling enough for the three of us. I rushed to her and put my head on her shoulder, wanting her to pet me and comfort me the way she had last night. She

held me for a moment, but then she drew back, laughing a little. "Come on, no more sulking, Salome. Look what a lus-
cious morning for us! We're going to view the progress on
the shrine to Diana."

As soon as I was dressed, Herodias bustled me into a litter that took us to the city square. The overseer showed us
around the half-built shrine. On the porch, pediments were
already in place for the columns to hold up the roof. "Do you
see the quality of this marble?" Herodias asked me. "I convinced Antipas to spare no expense to this shrine in your
honor. And on the roof, one of the statues of Diana's attendants is to have your face!—What's this?"

"This" was a ragged cloak draped over one of the pediments. "A worker must have left it, lady," said the overseer as
he pulled it away. Then he gasped and tried to put it back, but
it was too late.

### MURDERER

said red letters on the marble.

Pressing my hand to my mouth, I shrank back. But Herodias flew into a rage, screaming and stamping her foot. The
overseer bowed to her over and over, stammering promises to
find the "prankster" and hand him over to the guards. I crept
back into the litter, shuddering as if the day were cold.

"Salome, love. Salome, my pet." Slipping in beside me, Herodias patted my cheek. "How you suffer! You're so sensitive, just like me. But you have to understand, my dearest, that we had no choice."

"The head, staring!" I was desperate to make her understand. I held up a hand in front of my face. "It's as if it's *right there*."

But Herodias seemed determined not to understand. She reminded me, in a teasing tone, of the time I'd cried because I felt sorry for the roast suckling pig at a holiday dinner. Of course I'd been very little. I'd gotten used to roast pigs, hadn't I?

Herodias rattled on about how good life would be for the two of us now that the "baleful influence," as Magus Shazzar had put it, had been "occulted." We'd practice for a new performance of *Demeter and Persephone* and invite all the courtiers' wives to see it. We'd plan a shopping trip to Antioch, a stylish, lively city, "nicer than Rome."

But the head—the eyes, staring at me! I wanted to cry out. Herodias's cheery talk was an invisible shield, held up between her and my distress.

Herodias had the litter drop me off at the front steps of the palace, then went on to a social call on a nobleman's wife. I roamed through the colonnades and gardens, unable to sit still. In the main garden I glimpsed Leander, reading a scroll. I paused in the gateway, wondering whether to speak to him. But before I could step in, Leander glanced up and saw me. Jumping to his feet, he bowed and hurried out the other gate with his scroll half rolled.

The midday meal came and went, although I didn't eat it.

Now it was early afternoon. If this had been an ordinary day (if only I could return to the time of ordinary days!), I would visit Joanna.

Today I shrank from the thought of facing her, even as I longed to be with her. How could I explain what I'd done? I hadn't wanted the death of John the Baptizer, but last night, it had seemed necessary. I seemed to have wandered into a Greek tragedy, I thought. King Oedipus hadn't meant to kill his father and marry his mother, and yet he had committed those horrible acts.

At last I felt that I *must* see Joanna—I *must* make her understand. Pulling a shawl over my head (I felt a need to cover myself, although the day was hot), I hurried through the palace grounds to the steward's house.

Joanna's maid opened the door for me. She looked down at the floor as she said, "My mistress is away."

I glanced past Zoe through the atrium to the garden, where Joanna was reclining on her couch. I had feared this, but it was more painful than I expected. "Tell her I beg her to let me see her." As the maid did not step aside, I raised my voice. "I want to talk to her." In my own ears, my voice sounded like that of a spoiled child.

Joanna called to her maid, "Never mind, Zoe. I will speak with her after all."

At her tone of voice, my insides went cold. Still, I walked into the garden. Joanna gestured to a bench, but I didn't sit down. I went straight to her couch and dropped to my knees. "Joanna! Please understand. You have to understand—I only wanted to get away from Tiberias."

Joanna looked straight at me without speaking. There were smudges of weariness under her eyes.

I began to babble about Greek tragedies, and how frightened I was of my stepfather and mother, and what I'd intended when I danced at the banquet. I described how it felt to be a goddess, beyond the human limits of right and wrong—although of course I understood now that I wasn't really a goddess—

Still Joanna looked at me, stone-faced.

"It was the herb Gundi made me breathe," I pleaded. "I wasn't thinking straight. And then my mother—my mother made me feel that we were like gladiators, fighting together for our lives."

Joanna shook her head in disbelief. "First a goddess, then a gladiator."

"Oh, Joanna, my mother is like an evil enchantress! But now my eyes are opened, and I'll never be taken in by her again. It's like what you told me about repenting. I didn't want to look at what my mother was really like, but now I see."

I thought that Joanna's heart would soften if I talked of repenting, but she put her hands over her ears. "It is blasphemy for you to talk of repentance. Never mind Antipas, or Herodias, or Gundi's herbs. *You* have murdered God's messenger. *You* have taken away the hope of the people. You may be named after the Salome who saved the Jewish leaders, but you're nothing like her."

"I didn't want to harm the preacher!" I sobbed.

"Then why did you murder him? Antipas would have done whatever you asked! You could have asked to let John go free." Joanna closed her eyes, and her brow creased as if in pain. "Leave me." Then she opened her eyes and said, "No, stay a moment. I'll tell you how I spent the morning."

The deliberate way she spoke made me shiver, but I didn't move.

"As soon as I heard the news," said Joanna, "I sent my litter to the prison and my maid to the market to buy spices

and ointments for the burial. The litter bearers delivered the
Baptizer's body to the safe house, then returned to bring me
there. I couldn't help the other disciples anoint his body, but
I watched." She looked me in the face. "Fortunately, they'd
found the head on the palace trash heap, so they could wrap
the whole body together."

I was sitting in Joanna's garden, as I had many times. But
now I seemed to be outside it, as if I was shut out even while
I was there. The refreshing scented breeze, the peaceful mood,
was not for me.

Joanna's merciless voice went on. "No, I didn't have the
strength to help prepare the body, but at least I had money to
pay for a tomb. Not in accursed Tiberias, of course. They'll
bury him in Capernaum."

I couldn't speak. Joanna ended with quiet emphasis, "I
do not want you here with me." She closed her eyes again.

I left the steward's house, my face burning as if Joanna
had slapped me. I walked slowly at first, then faster and
faster, as if I could escape Joanna's ugly picture of me. Maybe
I was trying to run back to yesterday afternoon, when Joanna
had still been eager to see me. If only I had dropped my reckless, selfish plan and gone to Joanna for help instead!

By the time I reached the main garden, I was almost running. I was not Joanna's daughter; I was Herodias's daughter.

My mother *had* to comfort me now; she *had* to see how desperate I was. I dashed down the colonnade toward Herodias's suite.

I managed to hold myself together until I stood outside the doors to Herodias's sitting room. Her maid, Iris, opened the doors. "My lady isn't here."

I burst out crying, bending over as if I had cramps. Through my sobs, I heard a bright voice behind me. "What's all this?"

It was Herodias. I flung myself at her, clutching her so that she couldn't back away. I tried to speak, but my voice came out in a wordless wail.

Herodias gave an exasperated laugh. "What *is* all this, indeed? And where's Gundi when we need her?" As I sobbed and hiccuped, she took me by the arms and held me away from her. "Salome. Listen. I want you to go to the spa. Have a massage and a good long soak in the warm bath. Here. Iris will take you."

As I stumbled out the door, supported by the maid, Herodias added, "You must pull yourself together. It's time to put the unpleasantness behind us and move forward."

That night I lay awake thinking, I am a fool as well as a murderer. Hadn't I just told Joanna that Herodias was an evil enchantress? Hadn't I just declared, "I'll never be taken in by her again"? And yet, a few minutes later I ran to her for comfort!

My mother *ought* to love me as much as the goddess Demeter loved her daughter Persephone. But Herodias did not love me like that. She wasn't even my friend. She was never going to be my friend.

Worse, Herodias was making me into someone like herself. The night before, while I was dancing, I'd imagined I was casting a spell. I'd thought I was the goddess Aphrodite—what a twisted joke on me! I was a witless overgrown girl, blundering into murder.

I was tired, but I couldn't escape into sleep. I called Gundi to bring a sleeping potion, but she pretended not to hear me. I could hear her muttering on her pallet beside the door, "*Ach*, woe is me! Unlucky slave of a foolish girl!"

Finally I sank into a strange half sleep. I seemed to be lying at the bottom of a well—no, a dungeon cell. The air down there was as thick and foul as water in a sewer. Far above was just enough light to outline the grating. By my own doing, I was locked away from the world of fresh air and light and everything clean and good.

# TWENTY-TWO

# A CURSE ON THE HERODS

On Lake Tiberias one sunny day followed another and another, but I seemed to be in a gray fog. All my senses were dulled. Food tasted like lint, and music sounded like tuneless twanging.

I couldn't stand my own company, and the other people at court didn't seem to want it, either. Antipas avoided me as intently as he'd sought me out before. (Not that I wanted to be with *him*.) The painting of the nymph chased by a satyr, the one that had sent Herodias into an insane rage, disappeared from the main hall. In its niche appeared a portrait of the Tetrarch and his wife, dressed like Zeus and Hera, king and queen of the gods.

For all Antipas's robe-tearing on the night of the banquet, he now officially declared that the Baptizer's death was a good thing. He had an announcement explaining this sent out to all the towns of his realm. In the marketplace of Tiberias, I saw a copy fastened to the obelisk:

*Let it be known throughout Galilee and Perea: The dangerous rebel leader John, called the Baptizer, has been arrested and executed for the crimes of treason and inciting to treason. Hail to Prince Antipas, who has restored peace and order to the tetrarchy.*

I recognized the elegant lettering as Leander's.

I didn't dare try to visit Joanna again. I longed to talk to Leander, but he avoided me as carefully as Antipas did. If we happened to cross paths in the library, Leander turned his face aside, bowed, and hurried out of the room.

A small comfort was that Gundi went back to treating me much as she used to. After her high hopes and dreadful disappointment on the night of the banquet, Gundi must have reminded herself that there were worse things than belonging to a foolish girl. Scrubbing floors in a brothel, for instance, as Herodias had suggested.

Luckily for Gundi, Herodias was no longer in a mood to punish her and me by sending Gundi to the slave auction. She was the happiest person in the palace these days. At dinner she made Antipas chuckle with remarks that were both witty and flattering to him. He was seen visiting her suite at night again. Antipas no longer attended the Jewish prayer meeting every Sabbath or made any of his court attend.

Antipas agreed to appoint Herodias's brother, my uncle Agrippa, to the position of market master in Tiberias. Herodias looked forward eagerly to his arrival from Rome.

Meanwhile, Herodias hinted that she might persuade Antipas to send me back to the Temple of Diana in Rome instead of making a political marriage for me. Or perhaps I could be allowed to take up residence in Tiberias's new shrine to Diana. I pretended not to hear her. Herodias knew quite well that a disgraced maiden like myself could not serve the chaste goddess. If Antipas bribed the Temple to take me anyway, it would be only a sham.

When I thought back to my dream in the Temple of Diana, it seemed that some other girl—a much younger, more carefree girl—had dreamed it. These days, the only dreams I had were bad ones. I would find myself on the bank of a river, shrouded in chill fog, waiting for a ferry. I was trying to cross so that I could return something belonging to a man on the other side. The basket on my arm was heavy, and I longed to set it down, but I had to find the man first.

* * *

As the days went by, I dragged myself around the palace. I suppose I harbored some unreasonable hope, in spite of everything, that I could make Herodias care about how I was suffering. Then it would dawn on her that she'd done something dreadful, that life could not just go on as before.

Although Herodias paid no attention to my mood, she did include me in her activities. One morning some days after the banquet, she summoned me to her suite. She was holding auditions to choose the slaves to sing and play in her next dramatic performance.

While I watched glumly, a slave arrived from the guest suite with a message from Philip: he wished to speak with me in the east portico.

"Uncle Philip?" I roused myself from the chair where I was slumped. "I thought he'd already left Tiberias."

"What an idea!" Herodias's musical laugh rang out. "He wouldn't leave for Gaulanitis without saying goodbye to you." She gave me an arch look. "I think he was shocked— maybe a little intrigued—by your dance the other night." She dimpled at me, as if my dance were now a matter for teasing. "Maybe he hopes you'll dance for *him*."

I hadn't talked to Philip since the night of the banquet, and I shrank from the thought of looking him in the face. But

I let Gundi pin up my hair and went with her to the east portico.

Philip was waiting in a traveling cloak and boots. After greeting me, he made a few remarks about the weather. He asked politely if I was looking forward to seeing Jerusalem at the coming Feast of Booths.

I waited for Philip to tell me he was no longer interested in marriage with me. How would he phrase it in a polite way? "Now that I've gotten to know you somewhat . . ." It was really almost funny. I kept my eyes on the marble floor, but I was aware of his gaze. Maybe he was trying to decide if the listless girl before him was the same person as the murderous hussy who'd danced on Antipas's birthday.

Finally Philip said abruptly, "There's a terrible curse on us Herods—and I'm afraid we deserve it. Farewell." Before I could answer, he turned and hurried down the steps to where his attendants waited. The men disappeared in the direction of the docks.

Gundi accompanied me back to my room. "Now there's a decent prospect for a husband," she said. "Why didn't you smile at him? If you take my advice, you'll send him an encouraging note. I'm afraid he got the impression you weren't interested in him."

"Take your advice!" A surge of anger goaded my dull

spirits. "I'll never take your stupid barbarian advice again." I raised my hand to cuff her head, and she ducked. But then the anger drained away, and I hated only myself. Besides, it seemed like too much trouble to punish Gundi.

Later I went to the main garden by myself. I wasn't thinking of Leander, but there he was on a bench with his nose in a scroll. Judging from his dreamy expression, I thought he was far away in ancient Thebes, or Athens, or perhaps Troy. But then he looked up and saw me, and his face changed, as if he'd just noticed a scorpion. He rose, bowed, and started to hurry out of the garden.

"Wait!" I was determined to make him speak to me. After all, he was only a secretary.

He stopped and bowed again, expressionless, a servant waiting for an order.

"Leander, of all the people in Tiberias, you should understand that I had to . . . Don't, please don't just look at me. Speak."

Leander nodded, a servant accepting an order. "Understand? I understand some things," he began slowly. "I knew that Lady Herodias wanted the Baptizer dead. I knew—everyone in the palace knew—that the Tetrarch took an . . . *interest* in his stepdaughter." He stopped, his eyes on the flagstones.

"Go on," I said.

"Very well. I admit I hadn't expected Prince Antipas's stepdaughter to take advantage of his . . . interest in her. When she first began to dance, I couldn't believe it was her. She was not only seducing her stepfather, but doing it in front of a hall full of men."

I burned with shame, but I listened. I wanted so badly for him to talk to me.

"Then," continued Leander, "I thought, Is the young lady so desperate? Does she believe her only hope is to re-place her mother? Clearly, the Tetrarch thought this was her intention."

"But it wasn't; it *wasn't* what I meant to do!" I burst out.

Leander stopped speaking until I was silent again. Then he continued, "So the Tetrarch leaped at the chance. 'Half my kingdom'—obviously, he could hardly wait to take his step-daughter for his new wife."

"Yes, but I was deceiving him, don't you see?" I couldn't stand the way Leander was talking about me, as a person he had no connection with. "I know it wasn't decent, but I was possessed by the goddess—I had no will of my own. Please believe me!"

"Possessed by the goddess," Leander repeated in a flat voice. "*Hmm,* I didn't realize she was possessed. That excuses everything." He continued, "No, her real intention was much worse than either Antipas or I suspected. She seduced her stepfather, in public, in order to murder a good man."

"That wasn't my idea!" I pleaded. "Herodias—"

"Ah," interrupted Leander. "Now I understand. First she was possessed by Aphrodite, then by her mother." His polite, interested tone cut deeper than the heaviest sarcasm would have. After a pause, he finished, "I had thought Herodias's daughter was nothing like her mother, but I was wrong. She is a true Herod, a true descendant of her great-grandfather."

I felt breathless and sick, as if a stone had hit me in the stomach. "How dare you—I could call the guards. I could have you thrown in prison."

Leander looked at me. "Yes. The great-granddaughter of Herod could have my head on a platter, too."

I put up a hand to shield myself from his words. One more, I felt, and I would fall bleeding onto the path. But Leander was through with me. With a final bow, he left the garden.

I wandered up and down the paths, pulling off a leaf here and a blossom there. I noticed a gardener pretending not to look at me, and I realized he must be worried that I'd damage his plants. Sitting down on a bench, I twisted a lock of my hair until my scalp hurt. That pain seemed to balance the pain in my mind so that I could think.

Joanna had been right. Leander was right. I—not Aphrodite—had murdered John the Baptizer. I had *chosen* to use my power over Antipas to demand John's head. Herodias and Antipas were responsible, too, but that didn't mean I was less responsible.

I sat in the garden like a judge on the judgment seat, and I pronounced myself guilty. That was dreadful, but somehow satisfying.

What still disturbed me, strangely, was that no one would punish me. This was not like living in the middle of a tragic play after all. In a Greek tragedy, some kind of dreadful justice is done in the end.

Once, when we were still friends, Leander had tried to explain to me why he liked to watch tragic plays. Yes, it was harrowing to go through all the dying and suffering in a tragedy, he said, but at the end of the play he felt somehow satisfied. At the beginning of the play, the world had been out of kilter. The only way it could be set right was through terrible destruction.

At the time, I hadn't understood Leander, but now I began to see what he meant. To set things right, I ought to be punished for murdering the Baptizer. So should Antipas and Herodias. Especially since my stepfather and mother weren't suffering over John's death at all, but rather "putting the un-pleasantness behind them."

I longed to turn this story of the Herods into a proper tragedy. What if I poisoned our dinner one night? Gundi knew something about herbs and powders, and maybe I could bribe her with the promise of her freedom. The trouble with poison was, Antipas had a taster who took a bite of every dish before the Tetrarch ate it.

Besides, poison seemed too quiet and tidy for my feelings. I wanted some enormous force to wipe out us evil Herods. If I'd commanded an army, I would have ordered them to besiege Tiberias, burn the palace, and tear its walls stone from stone. Now, *that* would be satisfying.

One morning in the month after the banquet, I climbed to the upper terrace. The air over the lake was thick, but I could make out the cliffs of the eastern shore. That was the border dividing Galilee from Gaulanitis, the realm to which Philip had returned. I felt a pang, remembering his mild face. He didn't seem to be a real Herod. How had *he* escaped the family curse?

Movement at the north gate of the city caught my eye, and I saw a curtained litter leaving. Wasn't it the litter from

Steward Chuza's household? That was strange, because for months Joanna had barely had the strength to go to the hot springs.

When I asked Gundi, she confirmed that the steward's wife often took the litter out of Tiberias these days. She must be having a spurt of energy. The rumor was that she went to hear a new preacher, and he had a healing influence.

# TWENTY-THREE

# JOANNA DISAPPEARS

Now that I had no friends, I spent more time reading. At first I went to the palace library looking for my old favorites, Greek novels. But those romantic stories didn't hold my attention anymore. Then I tried to read Philo of Alexandria, the Jewish philosopher Leander admired, but I found his writings dry.

What suited me these days were the Jewish Scriptures. Not the psalms that Joanna loved, but the stories of times when this god had destroyed wicked people. Once he'd caused the earth to open and swallow up a clan who disobeyed him. Another time, he'd flooded the whole world in order to cleanse it and start over.

I especially liked the story of Samson. Samson was a hero of olden times, betrayed to the Philistines by the woman he loved and trusted. His enemies blinded him, imprisoned him, and made him grind grain like a donkey. When the Philistines were all gathered in their temple, celebrating their triumph over Samson, they brought him out to laugh at him. But Samson stood between the pillars that held up the temple and prayed to the Lord for strength to destroy his enemies. And he brought down the temple, burying himself along with thousands of Philistines.

What if John the Baptizer had done the same in the Tetrarch's scarlet-pillared audience hall? I imagined the walls of Antipas's marble palace cracking and crumbling and the gold-leaf roof shattering on top of the pile. Antipas's expensive paintings and statues and mosaics, his carefully tended gardens—all crushed down into the prisons, the torture chambers, and the dungeons. The Tetrarch, his wife, and his stepdaughter would be smashed in the rubble like slugs.

While I dreamed of destruction, the time of the Jewish harvest festival, the Feast of Booths, came around. Although Antipas seemed to have lost his enthusiasm for observing the Jewish customs, it was still important for him to be seen in Jerusalem at the high festival. So he'd take his court south for the celebration, as he had in past years. Only Steward Chuza would stay behind to manage things.

At first I was determined to stay behind, too. Why would I want to spend two days in the carriage each way with Herodias? On the other hand, there was nothing much to keep me in Tiberias. Besides, I felt drawn to see such a great gathering of the Jewish faithful. Supposedly we Herods were Jews, ruling over Jews, but I knew almost nothing about this ancient faith. I would go to Jerusalem and see.

During the journey, Herodias went on at length about how Antipas (not any of his brothers and certainly not Pontius Pilate) was the rightful ruler of Judea, including Jerusalem. When we reached Jerusalem, she pointed out a tower looming over the compound of the Great Temple. "That's the Castle of Antonia, the palace rebuilt by my grandfather King Herod. In justice, the castle should be our residence in Jerusalem. But of course it's been taken over by the Romans."

A massive outer wall protected the Temple grounds. We passed through a tunnel-like gate in the wall and came out into the Court of the Gentiles. This was like an enormous marketplace, thronged with tens of thousands of people. "Make way for the Tetrarch of Galilee," shouted Antipas's guards, and the crowds parted to let us cross the court.

A gate in the inner wall led to the Women's Court. From there, Antipas and his entourage climbed a set of semi-circular steps and disappeared through the gate into the Men's Court.

The moment I stepped into the Women's Court, where no non-Jews were allowed, I felt the holiness of the place. There was wonder and joy on the faces around me, and I saw a woman kneeling to kiss the pavement.

Herodias and I, with our attendants, went up into the women's gallery for a better view. The Levite priests appeared on the semicircular steps and sang psalms. Great golden lamps shone around the outer court, and trumpets blared as the priests poured libations from golden pitchers.

The woman next to me was a stranger, but she beamed at me as if I were her niece. "Is this your first Feast of Booths, my dear? It's a great blessing to be here, isn't it?"

I smiled and nodded to return her kindness. But I thought, It *would* be a great blessing, if only I belonged here. I gazed around at the other women crowding the gallery, lifting children up to see. There was joy on their faces, too.

I glanced at Herodias, who was buffing her fingernails. She didn't belong here, either, but she didn't care. Anyway, it was no comfort to be like my mother. I felt so lonely that my throat ached. I wished for the Feast of Booths to be over so that we could leave Jerusalem.

Journeying back to Tiberias, we entered the city late one afternoon. As our procession stopped at the palace steps, I looked up to see Steward Chuza in the portico. Of course he would be there, to welcome the Tetrarch home. But the strange thing was, he was *sitting* at the top of the steps. "Is the man ill?" asked Herodias, stepping out of the carriage.

No—Chuza was drunk. We could see that much when he tried to stand up.

Antipas was angry, then worried. He questioned his steward, who tried awkwardly to distract him by asking about the Tetrarch's journey. Finally it came out: Chuza was distraught because his wife, Joanna, had gone off to follow the new preacher.

Just like that! It took my breath away.

The courtiers were breathless, too. They crowded the portico around the steward, who stood wavering in front of Antipas.

"Didn't you forbid her?" demanded Antipas.

"Joanna didn't ask my permission, my lord," said Chuza miserably. "She left before dawn. When I woke up, there was only a letter. She said the Rabbi had healed her, and she was going to follow him as a disciple."

"That's ridiculous," said Antipas. "A woman can't be a disciple. And wives can't just do as they please."

Wives can't do as they please? I glanced at Herodias. Chuza stared at Antipas, too drunk to conceal his amazement. The Tetrarch scowled, cleared his throat, and changed the subject. "I thought it was the mineral baths that were healing your wife."

"Undoubtedly it was, my prince." Chuza bowed unsteadily. "Our gratitude toward my lord is boundless," he added in a mumble.

Antipas gave a disgusted snort. "Never mind. Tell me what you've found out about the new preacher."

Making an effort to pull himself together, the steward reported what his information gatherers had told him. "His name is Yeshua bar Joseph, my prince, from Nazareth. He goes around among the Jewish towns, often on the lake—Bethsaida, Magdala, Capernaum. He draws large crowds. He *may* have been in Jerusalem part of the time you were there, during the Feast of Booths. According to our contacts among the Temple leaders, there was a Galilean preacher named Yeshua in Jerusalem, stirring up the people. The Temple leaders nearly arrested him but changed their minds at the last moment. But of course Yeshua is a common Jewish name, and there are many preachers."

Antipas waved a hand, as he often did when Chuza was giving him too many little facts. "Does he preach against me?"

"Not exactly." The steward, who usually plodded methodically from one fact to another, looked dismayed. He must have come to a fact he'd rather not report. The courtiers pressed closer to hear.

"Well?" Antipas leaned toward him. "Cough it up."

"One source reported that he referred to my prince as 'that fox.'"

I raised my hand to hide a smile. Chuza wouldn't have said that if he were sober. Antipas liked to think of himself as a mighty bull.

"Does he preach treason?" asked Antipas in a sharper tone.

"Not exactly," said Chuza again. "He tells the people, 'The kingdom of heaven is at hand.' That could mean many things."

Antipas's eyebrows drew together. "Whatever it means, have our men watch him closely. Report everything he says."

I hadn't seen Joanna since the day after the Baptizer's death, and I had no reason to think that she'd ever want to speak to me again. Still, knowing that she was gone made Tiberias

seem like a truly hopeless place. I hated the airy rooms and
marble colonnades of the palace, the gardens with flowering
vines and singing birds. As though I were a scuttling night
creature, something was pulling me toward the darkness underneath Antipas's magnificent halls.

One afternoon, when most of the palace was dozing, I
wrapped myself in a shawl and pulled it forward to hide my
face. Pushing a few extra bangles onto my wrist, I sneaked
out of the women's quarters.

I wasn't sure where the entrance to the prison was, but I
thought it must be beyond the kitchens, which were beyond
the far end of the great dining hall. The soldiers' barracks and
the stables were on that side of the palace, I knew.

As I passed through the doorway from the dining hall, I
had the sense of peering behind the scenery in a theater. In
the corridor leading past the kitchens, there were no Greek
statues, no sumptuous wall hangings, no gilded lamp stands.
The kitchen slaves, sweating in their drab tunics, looked up
briefly as I passed.

The corridor ended in a gate to the soldiers' courtyard.
The gate was guarded, but the guards dozed in the midday
heat. I slipped past them. In the deep archway a small, iron-
bound door hid a stairway. The guard at this doorway was

awake, and I was afraid he would question me. But he took the bangle I silently offered as though taking bribes was a regular part of his job.

I had to pick my way carefully down the rough steps in the feeble light from a lamp here and there on the walls. At the bottom of the steps there was a corridor with a row of cells. The jailer was leaning against the bars of the first cell, chatting with the prisoner inside.

"My lady," the jailer greeted me. Of course, he knew from my clothes that I wasn't someone's maid. But I had the feeling he knew who I was—or maybe he only thought he knew? "Did you wish to visit—" He gestured at the prisoner.

I tried to disguise my voice at least with a sort of hoarse growl. "No, I want to see . . . Show me the place where the Baptizer died." I held out a bangle.

The jailer looked at the bangle longingly, but he shook his head. Thinking he wanted more, I pulled off another bangle, but he held up his hand. "Keep your silver, lady. I'll show you." Taking a torch from the wall, he led me down the corridor.

I held a corner of my shawl over my nose and mouth to filter the foul air. Some of the prisoners slumped listlessly in a corner; others groaned. Some of them stared at me as if they were seeing a vision.

The jailer stopped before the last cell, holding up his torch. He nodded at me. "The holy man was in here." There was nothing in the cell except a brown stain on the stone floor. "I was going to clean this up, soon as I had a chance," said the jailer.

Grim as it was, this was not the dark, cramped place I'd expected. "Wasn't the Baptizer kept in a dungeon?"

"Ah—yes, he was, when he first came here. Of course that wasn't where he died, but if my lady would like to take a look—" The jailer led me down another set of steps to a pit in the rock, covered with an iron grate.

I gazed and gazed into the black hole. Why had I come here? I'd had some hazy idea of finding a place ugly and evil enough for me. I'd found it, all right. This foul pit was a true and fitting monument to the reign of the Herods.

"My lady?" The jailer's voice, puzzled, broke into my thoughts. "There's not much more to see. No prisoner down there at the moment."

What had I thought I was going to do—crawl into the dungeon? I could hardly expect the jailer to let me do that. Pulling myself together with an effort, I climbed the steps back to the row of cells.

Now the prisoners were expecting me, and the able-bodied ones jumped up and called through the bars. "Lady

Joanna," begged the nearest prisoner, "take a message to my old mother?"

I turned around, as if Joanna could be standing behind me. Oh! The prisoner thought *I* was Joanna. "I'm sorry—I'm not—"

"A blanket, please, kind Lady Joanna," called another man. "My friend is sick, and it's so cold down here."

"Don't let them hurt me, Lady Joanna," pleaded still another. "I wasn't the one who wrote 'Murderer,' I swear; how could I, gracious lady? I can't write!"

Their pleas came at me like a shower of pebbles. I looked helplessly at the jailer.

"I've told you and told you," he growled at the prisoners, "*don't* say my lady's name!"

They all, including the jailer, thought I was Joanna. They didn't understand that I was an evil person who belonged in the black pit below. Well, I supposed I could pretend to be Joanna long enough to do a few things for them.

"Here," I said to the jailer. I pulled a bangle off my wrist again. "This will buy fresh bread, watered wine, and blankets for them. You must really use the silver for that, or—"

I didn't know quite what to threaten the jailer with, but he nodded. "Don't worry, lady. I'll do as you say. I've repented." He shook his head wonderingly. "One thing leads to another."

The jailer was so right: one thing leads to another. For the prisoner with the old mother, I took a message to the slum outside the city. I found the woman in a lean-to with four little boys. She wasn't so old—no older than Herodias, probably—but she'd lost most of her teeth, and her hair was gray.

"Your son says, don't sell any of his boys," I told her. "Wait till he gets out of prison."

"Easy for him to say," she mumbled. "How will I feed the children? The last time we had money was when the Tetrarch returned to Tiberias and scattered alms. Nikos here"—she pointed to the oldest boy—"managed to grab one of the coins."

"Someone stepped on my hand, but I didn't let go," said the boy. He was as serious and dignified as a rabbi, in spite of his patched tunic and the freckles on his nose.

As I looked at the boy, I remembered the evening when I'd entered Tiberias for the first time. That day, the beggars in the square had been only background to Antipas and the important people (especially me) in his entourage. Now one of those beggar children stood before me, and I understood that Nikos was the truly important person in that scene. Antipas's only purpose in tossing coins to the crowd was to feel powerful and generous. Nikos, diving after the coins, aimed to save himself and his family from starving.

When I asked why the father was in prison, the grandmother explained that he'd foolishly lent money to a neighbor. Instead of repaying the debt, the neighbor had reported
the father to Antipas's guards for bribing a palace official.
Nothing had been proven, but they kept him in prison.

So I promised to see what I could do to get the father released. Meanwhile, I left another silver bangle with the
grandmother.

On my way back to the palace, I stopped in the market
and bought several simple bracelets and rings. The jeweler
tried to sell me more expensive pieces, assuring me that my
credit at the palace was good for gold and precious stones.
"Princess Herodias (may she live long and prosper!) wishes
to see her daughter properly attired." But I wanted only small
items that could easily be bartered for food and clothes by
common people.

This kind of thing went on for several days. Every time I
thought I was through with pretending to be Joanna, I discovered more work to be done. For instance, I sent Gundi to
the courthouse to inquire about the prisoner accused of
painting MURDERER on the shrine to Diana.

Gundi reported back that the man in prison was almost
certainly the one who'd painted the treasonous sign. (In
spite of what he'd told me, he could read and write well

enough to copy a few letters.) But whether he was innocent or guilty, the quickest way to get him released from prison was to bribe a judge. For that matter, the quickest way to get the father accused of bribery released was also to bribe a judge.

Had Joanna gone that far, breaking the law in order to do justice? I couldn't ask her, so I would have to decide for myself. And right or wrong, I had to admit it was a pleasure to break the laws of Herod Antipas.

# TWENTY-FOUR

# JOANNA REAPPEARS

One afternoon I stood on the lower terrace, looking out over Lake Tiberias. It had been several days, I realized, since I'd thought of drowning myself in the lake. There were many other things to think about now. For instance, I needed to go back to the jeweler and buy a really handsome piece, maybe a gold tiara. You couldn't expect a judge to release a prisoner for a mere silver bangle.

Footsteps crunched on the sandy path, and I turned to see Leander. I expected him to flinch at the sight of me and hurry off the terrace. Instead, he approached me and bowed. "Good afternoon, Miss Salome."

"Good afternoon," I said, wondering why he was speaking to me now. "What is it?"

As I waited for him to speak, Leander glanced aside, embarrassed. "Miss Salome," he said, "I have been most discourteous. It was some time ago that my sister and mother sent you their heartfelt thanks for your gracious gift. Please believe that they are grateful."

"Gift?" For a moment, I didn't know what he was talking about. "Oh! The bronze lamp." It seemed like a lifetime ago that a girl named Salome had bought that wedding present in the market. "I'm happy that they liked it." I waited, because he seemed to be working himself up to say something else.

Leander finally spoke, haltingly, as if the words pained him. "I wish to beg Miss Salome's pardon for . . . for what I said the last time we spoke. It was wrong of me and rude. My only excuse, perhaps, is that I didn't want to admit how deeply I've betrayed my own standards."

"You mean working for Antipas?" I asked in surprise. "But you're stuck. You have to earn your sisters' dowries."

"Not by serving an evil master," said Leander. He sighed. "I made one feeble attempt to get away—I asked Tetrarch Philip, before he left, to hire me as his secretary. But it seems that Philip can't afford a secretary. Besides, he writes his own letters, and he doesn't have any Deep Thoughts."

"That's what I liked about Philip," I said, daring to smile at Leander.

"I too." An answering smile twitched his mouth. "By the way, I thought you might want to know that you have the Tetrarch worried."

"Worried?" As far as I could tell, Antipas had put me out of his mind entirely. He didn't seem to see me when we passed in the halls or even on the rare occasions when I dined with him and Herodias.

"Actually, he *thinks* he's worried about Lady Joanna. Although she no longer lives in Tiberias, Antipas hears reports that she magically appears here and there, comforting the Tetrarch's prisoners and helping the poor."

"Oh," I said.

"Your secret is safe with me," said Leander. "I won't tell anyone that you've repented." Bowing again, he left the terrace.

I hadn't repented, of course. I was only a murderer who'd somehow gotten caught up in doing the kinds of things Joanna used to do. Still, I was glad to be on speaking terms with Leander, even under false pretenses. It brightened my days just to know that I might run into him in the library or gardens and exchange a few friendly words.

Herodias, on the other hand, had gotten out of the habit

of confiding in me now that she and Antipas were in such harmony. I was surprised one morning when Iris brought a message from Herodias: she'd ordered a carriage to take us up into the hills, "just the two of us with a picnic lunch."

So just the two of us (plus a large basket of delicacies, a table, chairs, and awning, Iris and Gundi to wait on us, the carriage driver, and a dozen guards in case of bandits) drove up to the highest point above the city. Sitting under the striped awning, I gazed down on a fish pool–sized Lake Tiberias. From here, it didn't look big enough to drown in. Anyway, I thought with a smile, it was just as well I'd given up planning to drown myself. It wasn't a practical plan—I was too good a swimmer.

"My daughter"—Herodias's voice broke into my thoughts— "the time for dallying is done. You must make up your mind to be married, for your own security as well as mine."

I looked at her in alarm. "I *won't* marry the Nabatean prince."

"Who said anything about the Nabatean prince?" (*She* had, the last time she mentioned my marriage plans. But never mind.) "I'm talking, of course, about Philip of Gaulanitis. He was a bit put off by your behavior, it's true, but I'm doing my best to mend that bridge. I sent him your portrait."

I stared at her. "What portrait? What are you talking about?"

It turned out that Herodias had found the picture of a nymph who looked exactly like me in a storage room. "I suspected that Antipas wouldn't want to actually destroy that expensive painting." She'd had the picture wrapped and sent to Philip with a perfumed note. "It can't hurt to remind Philip how pretty you are. Now if you'll follow up with a friendly letter . . ."

Was Herodias stark raving mad? While I was struggling for words, she put a finger up to her lips. "Listen, daughter, before you speak. I've made a dreadful discovery."

My first thought was that she'd found out about my visits to the prison or about how I was channeling Antipas's money into jewelry only to give it away. But those things were foolish rather than "dreadful," at least from Herodias's point of view.

"If it's true," Herodias went on, "I am not safe in Tiberias, and neither are you. You must go, marry, and make another home for yourself. Then, if worst comes to worst, you can offer me refuge."

"Refuge from *what*?"

"Perhaps it isn't true—how could it be true, after all? And

yet, how could there be more than one such demon of a man?"

It dawned on me that what she was saying was somehow connected with John. "You mean—"

"The new preacher, Yeshua, the one Joanna went to follow. Chuza tells Antipas that they say he's"—her voice sank to a whisper—"John the Baptizer come back to life."

"What!" My heart started pounding as if I'd hiked all the way up the hill from the palace.

"Of course this couldn't be true," Herodias hurried on, "because it seems he's the Baptizer's cousin. To be exact, Chuza says Yeshua's mother and John's mother are cousins. But if he *is* the Baptizer, that would explain a great deal: the strange fascination this man has for Antipas. Joanna's magical powers—how she's able to appear at will in Tiberias, for instance, even through prison walls."

Herodias talked on and on, but I hardly heard anything else she said during our outing. I couldn't wait to get back to the palace and think by myself. *John the Baptizer come back to life.* The words repeated themselves in my head, like a resounding gong.

Later, back at the palace, I felt a strange mixture of fear and hope. If John the Baptizer had come back to life, then I wasn't really a murderer, was I? Then there was no tragedy.

"Gundi," I said, stopping suddenly on the grand staircase. "Go to the docks; get us a place on a boat tomorrow."

"One of the Tetrarch's fleet?" she asked. "I don't have the authority—"

"No, not a palace boat." I didn't want to let anyone know where I was going. "It doesn't matter what kind of boat as long as it's sailing to a place where I can find the new preacher. You've heard his name? Yeshua."

Gundi went off protesting about proper behavior (although how could I behave any more improperly than I already had?) and grumbling about having to traipse all the way down to the waterfront. But I thought she was a bit curious to see this new preacher herself.

The next morning, I dressed in Gundi's spare tunic and shawl, and she and I walked past the palace guards and down through the city to the public docks. At the lakeside, the breeze carried the pungent odor of the fishing nets spread over the pebbly shore.

Stopping in front of a fishing boat, Gundi turned to me. "Here we are, Miss Salome." She looked satisfied. It was the expression she wore when she'd followed my orders but was sure I wouldn't like the result.

Certainly this boat was no pleasure barge. It was a grubby fishing boat, already half full of peasants. "Are you sure they're following the new preacher?" I asked Gundi.

Not quite trusting her, I also asked the boatman, who was helping an elderly man into the boat. The boatman spoke Aramaic with a sprinkling of common Greek, and I could barely understand him. But when I said, "Yeshua bar Joseph?" he nodded vigorously and took the coins I held out.

I'd been rather proud of my disguise as a commoner. But now that I was surrounded by Galilean peasants, I could see that I didn't look anything like them. I was taller than all the women and girls, taller even than many of the men. My chambermaid's tunic and shawl, which had looked shabby in the palace, were still of finer cloth and cleaner than these people's clothes. I was cleaner, too. The people in the boat wouldn't even be allowed in the public baths if they tried to go there.

I caught part of a discussion behind me about who the "Greek girl" and the woman with her might be. Servants of a noble house, they agreed. I had to admit that was a good guess.

Our boat was full. The boatman's helper cast off, and the

sail filled with the warm, moist breeze. The city of Tiberias shrank behind us. As the boatman steered the craft up the middle of the lake, a town at the northern tip came in sight.

"Bethsaida," called the boatman, pointing. He assured the passengers that Rabbi Yeshua had been seen here just the day before. "He fed a whole crowd of people."

The hull of the boat scraped the pebbly bottom, and the passengers scrambled off. As I waded ashore, I thought, Soon I'll stand before the preacher. My heart beat faster. If he's John come back to life, I'll know. But surely he'll know who I am, too. Would he strike me dead on the spot? He must be a man of great power, this preacher who'd healed Joanna after many skilled physicians had failed.

"The Rabbi isn't here any longer!" It was the first man off the boat, running back from the town. "They say he left for Capernaum."

"Capernaum!" They all turned back to the boat, clamoring to be taken across the lake. The boatman could have demanded more money for taking them farther, but he smiled and shrugged. "That Rabbi Yeshua, he's a slippery fish."

As I waded back to the boat, I was relieved, but also disappointed, that my moment to meet the preacher hadn't yet come. A while later, watching the town of Capernaum draw closer and closer, I remembered something Joanna had told

me the last time I saw her. She'd said that John the Baptizer
would be buried here. I raised my eyes beyond the docks and
the clusters of houses, past the Jewish assembly hall, to the
hills. His tomb would be among the rocks up there.

At the thought, the grisly image I'd pushed out of my
mind since Antipas's banquet came back, more vivid than
life. The platter seemed to float in front of me, offering its
gray-faced head. Then I imagined a tomb opening up in the
hills, the great round stone rolling away from the mouth by
itself. My hands felt clammy, and I wiped them on my shawl.

By the time we docked at Capernaum, fear was on me
like an illness. I could hardly make myself leave the boat. But
with the other passengers, I climbed the steep streets to join
a crowd below the assembly building. The town was shabby,
but the assembly hall was a fine basalt structure with gray
marble columns.

Gundi kept her arm locked in mine as the crowd pushed
us this way and that. I craned my neck, wondering if Joanna
was here, hoping and fearing to meet her. I did see from a distance a woman I recognized, but it was the banquet dancer,
holding a little girl. She looked younger without all the paint
on her face. I felt a stab of regret—if only *she* had danced at
the banquet!

Murmurs ran through the crowd: the Rabbi was in the

assembly hall, teaching. Soon he would come out and give us all bread. Gazing up the broad white steps, I watched the Jewish men step out of the shade of the building into the sunlight. I looked at each one and wondered, Is this the Rabbi? What about this one? I suppose I expected to see a man in camel-hair cloth, like John the Baptizer.

Whether Rabbi Yeshua was John or not, I thought, if he was a prophet, he'd know who I was as soon as he caught sight of me. Maybe he'd call down lightning from the sky to consume me with fire, like a sacrificed calf. And maybe that would be a fitting end to the tragedy of Salome.

As we waited, I heard two men arguing behind me. "How could Rabbi Yeshua be John the Baptizer come back to life?" demanded one of them. "He didn't appear out of nowhere—he grew up in Nazareth, after all." The second man claimed that John's spirit might have fallen upon Yeshua. "Just the way the spirit of the prophet Elijah came upon his disciple Elisha, after Elijah was taken up in the chariot of fire."

I didn't know this Jewish legend, and I wondered what the rest of it was. But then disappointing news rippled through the crowd: Rabbi Yeshua had left the assembly hall by the back way and gone to a friend's house. He wouldn't speak to the people again today.

"I could have told you this would happen," said Gundi.

I was too let down to be angry with her. I couldn't believe this was the end of my day of hope and fear. I couldn't even whirl on my heel and stalk back to the docks, because the crowd was so tightly packed.

Now the men behind me were talking about John's death. As I listened, I realized that they hadn't believed a word of Antipas's official explanation, announced and posted throughout Galilee and Perea. Probably no one had believed it.

Both the men obviously knew the story of John's death, and they rivaled each other to give the juiciest details. "And that she-demon Herodias was determined to kill him, so she ordered her slut of a daughter—"

"—to dance for Antipas—and a whole hall full of men!— stark naked—"

It wasn't like that, I wanted to tell them. But it *was* quite a bit like that.

"They say the guard didn't strike hard enough with the sword the first time, so—"

Gundi gave me a frightened look, and she motioned with her head back toward the docks. I felt sick and sweaty. I wanted badly to get away, but the crowd hemmed me in.

"—and when they brought that little slut the holy man's head, she kissed it on the lips!"

"No!" The word burst out of my mouth. I didn't dare to

turn around. My heart thudded, and I thought, Now they'll guess who I am. Will they spit at me? Stone me?

Probably the people outside the assembly hall only wondered what was the matter with that Greek maid. The men behind me didn't know I was Herodias's "slut of a daughter" in their story. But I felt my guilt was as clear as if I held the silver platter in my hands again.

"Mad to come to Capernaum!" muttered Gundi. "Without any escort whatsoever—without even litter bearers!" Hauling me by the wrist, she struggled through the crowd.

Frantically I tried to push after her downhill toward the boat. But it was like trying to run through a deep pool in the baths. My steps were nightmare slow. I heard mutters around me. No doubt they were saying only, "Watch who you're shoving," but to me it sounded like, "Murderer!" My wrist slipped from Gundi's sweaty hand, and I lost sight of her.

I was panting with fear by the time a woman in front of me seized my arms. In my blind panic, it took me a moment to hear her saying my name. "Salome. *Eirene,* peace, Salome."

# TWENTY-FIVE

# A SECOND CHANCE?

I knew this woman. "Joanna," I said slowly. Although I'd been looking for her, I was amazed to see her. She was truly healed. There she stood, confident on her feet even in the jostling crowd.

Joanna looked quite different standing upright. And the lines of strain were gone from her face.

"Don't be afraid, Salome. Come this way, out of the crowd."

I followed her into a side street, and we sat down on a low wall. "Did you come to hear Rabbi Yeshua?" she asked.

I nodded. "Is he . . . John the Baptizer come back to life?"

"No." Her eyes searched my face. "You were hoping . . ." She looked unutterably sad, and I realized with a shock that she was reflecting my own sadness. It really was that bad. I *was* a murderer, as the red letters painted on the shrine had told me. Nothing could change that.

"But still, there's hope," Joanna rushed on. "I know why people are saying he's the Baptizer, because he's carrying on what the Baptizer began. Oh, Salome! I wish you'd heard the Rabbi. It's not just what he says; it's *him*. But today, maybe it doesn't matter that you didn't hear him. Maybe the important thing was for me to hear his message and finally take it in. Now I can pass it on to you."

I didn't understand what Joanna was talking about, but I was content to sit with her. I'd missed her so much.

"Yes. It must be that you and I met today for a purpose," Joanna went on. "Because I was sure I'd never forgive you. I thought I was *right* to hate you. Even when I heard that you'd repented, I hardened my heart toward you."

"But I didn't repent," I said. It hurt me to say so, but I had to be honest with Joanna. "Leander thought I'd repented, and I suppose he spread it around, but it's not true. I only did some things you would have done in Tiberias if you hadn't left."

Joanna gave me an odd look. "My dear silly Salome, what do you think 'repent' means? But never mind!" she rushed on. "Before anything else, I want you to know"—her voice shook, and she swallowed as if she were tasting bitter medicine—"I want to take back the cruel words I said to you last time we met. Then, I wanted you to suffer." Taking my hand, she looked into my eyes. "I see that you *are* suffering, Salome."

She was speaking straight to my heart. I trembled, and tears burned my eyes.

"The Rabbi says we have to forgive each other," said Joanna. "Do you understand?"

I wanted to—I strained to understand—but I didn't. I shook my head.

"It's because the Lord is so merciful to us. That's what Rabbi Yeshua says. He says we can't receive the Lord's mercy unless we're merciful to others." She smiled, as though it were a delightful joke on us. "It's true! I've felt it."

"Is that how you were healed?" I asked wonderingly.

Joanna looked puzzled, then smiled again. "You mean, of my wasting illness. No. The Rabbi just—" She laughed, holding out her hands palms up to show bewilderment. "Blessing after blessing! This man scatters blessings around like a sower scattering grain."

Joanna talked on eagerly, telling me about the amazing things that happened in the presence of Rabbi Yeshua. One of his disciples, a woman named Mary, had urged Joanna to ask the Rabbi for healing. "Mary said she was tormented by demons for years before she met the Rabbi. I could hardly believe it—she's so peaceful now. But I do believe, because here *I* am." She laughed and stamped her feet to show how well they worked.

Joanna said she was staying with Mary in Magdala, another town on the shore of the lake. When I told her how crushed Chuza was that she'd left him, she shook her head. "I tried to tell him. I tried to get him to come with me to hear Rabbi Yeshua. But Chuza is so devoted to the Tetrarch, he can't see anything else." She gave a sad laugh. "He's married to Antipas, not to me. Thank the Lord, I have an inheritance, so I don't need to live on the Tetrarch's accursed land any longer."

We sat in silence for a moment. I felt dazed and very tired, but peaceful.

Joanna asked, "What about you, Salome? You're to marry Philip of Gaulanitis, aren't you?"

"Philip went back across the lake to his lands." Turning to her, I burst out, "Let me come to Magdala with you!"

"Oh, my dear." Joanna looked at me tenderly. "I would

be so glad if you could follow the Rabbi with me. But the Tetrarch wouldn't let you go: he'd send soldiers to bring you back. That would be very dangerous for Rabbi Yeshua and his friends, and it wouldn't do you any good." She hesitated, looking away. "Also—I know the Rabbi could forgive you for his cousin's death—*he* could do anything. But I'm afraid it might be asking too much . . . Some of the Rabbi's followers used to be John's disciples."

"Yes, I see," I said in a shaky voice. What I saw, in my mind's eye, was myself forever holding the platter with the gruesome evidence. Being forgiven didn't mean that I hadn't caused the prophet's death. Maybe, in years to come, the story of the Baptizer's death would be the only thing that anyone remembered about me. "I'm an accursed Herod; that's my fate."

Silently Joanna took my hand again and held it, sharing my heavy sadness. After a moment she said, "Take heart, Salome. I believe you can still turn your life around. Philip isn't a 'Herod,' not in the way you mean. When you're the wife of a kind and just ruler, you'll have the power to do much good. How I've wished that Chuza had been Philip's steward instead of Antipas's!"

Joanna had a vision of me, or rather of how I could be. I strained to see her vision, so far from my own idea of myself.

"You sound as hopeful about Philip as Herodias—she wants me to write him a 'friendly letter'! I'm sure he doesn't want me for his wife now."

Joanna's eyebrows went up. "Did he say so? Everyone seemed to think he liked you very much. Did you tell him how you came to dance at the banquet?"

I gazed at her, too surprised to answer. I hadn't even thought of trying to explain to Philip. I hadn't thought it would make a difference. While I was puzzling, I noticed Gundi hurrying toward us from the main street. "Miss Salome," she called in an outraged tone, "the boat has left without us."

I'd forgotten about Gundi. All this time she'd been looking for me—and fearing, I realized, that I'd been torn apart by the crowd. If anything happened to me while she was escorting me, of course she'd be harshly punished. Without thinking, I said something I'd never heard an owner say to a slave: "I'm sorry."

"*Sorry* won't mend broken eggs," Gundi snapped. Then it sank into her what I'd just said, and she stared at me, openmouthed. I giggled, and so did Joanna. If the followers of Rabbi Yeshua always laughed this much, I thought, it would be worth following him just for the fun.

"You'd better go now," said Joanna. "Storms can come

up on the lake in a hurry." She walked down to the docks with us and helped me find another boat back to Tiberias. Joanna and I hugged, promising to write.

On the way home, a letter—not to Joanna—began to form itself in my head:

*To Philip, Tetrarch of Gaulanitis, from Salome, ward of Antipas and daughter of Herodias, greetings.*

Joanna was right: my best chance to escape being a "Herod" was to marry Philip. What if he wouldn't marry me? He *must*. If somehow, by any means, I could get him to marry me, then I could turn my life around later, when I was safely in Caesarea Philippi.

But no. I had to start turning my life around now, with this letter. I knew exactly the kind of letter Herodias wanted me to write, full of flattery and tantalizing hints of passion. But I would not write Philip that way. I would tell him straight out what had happened the night of the banquet, with no excuses. And I would humbly ask to begin my new life—by sharing it with him.

# TWENTY-SIX

# BEYOND TRAGEDY

The next morning I labored with pen and ink and papyrus to explain myself to Philip. I didn't try to justify myself, but I asked for his understanding. I told how Antipas had stalked me and of my scheme to escape Tiberias and return to the Temple of Diana. I told him how Herodias had first terrified me before the banquet and then, after my dance, appealed to my pity as her daughter. I described how it had seemed right, at the time, to use my moment of power as Herodias demanded.

At the end of the letter, I begged Philip's forgiveness. I admired him as a just ruler and wished to share his life. I would be honored and grateful, I wrote, if I could become his wife after all.

When the letter was rolled and sealed, I went to the palace office and gave it to Leander. "Will you put this in the pouch when the courier leaves for Gaulanitis?"

"Of course, Miss Salome. May I take the liberty of saying, I'm happy for your good fortune, that you'll escape to Philip's realm. Although I'll be sorry to give up your company."

"Thank you," I said, embarrassed. I suppose it was obvious why I was writing to Philip. "But what makes you so sure that Philip still wants me for his wife? Or that he'll believe that I want to turn my life around? Did you know that Herodias sent him an indecent picture of me?"

Leander swallowed a smile. "Yes, I knew about that, but I don't see how it would hurt. Philip may be a just ruler, but he's also a human being. Who could blame him for choosing a beautiful wife?"

I wasn't convinced, but I felt a little more hopeful.

As I went back to my room, my thoughts turned to Leander. It seemed that there was no end to repentance. Again and again, I found myself seeing other people in a new light. I realized now that I had the power to release Leander from his bondage. Why hadn't I understood this before?

Probably, I was ashamed to admit, because I selfishly didn't want him to leave.

After selling a few of the costly knickknacks from my room, I sought out Leander again. I found him in the library, sitting on his favorite bench under the east windows. I remembered the first time I'd spoken to him, in the atrium of our house in Rome. "What are you reading, secretary?" I asked.

"Miss Salome." Rising to bow to me, Leander answered, "I'm re-reading Aeschylus's tragedy *Agamemnon*. It's about a king murdered by his wife." He paused, then added, "In this play, the whole royal house is under a curse."

I nodded. The palace of Herod Antipas was a fitting place to read such a play. "And what about philosophy—are you still studying philosophy?"

"I'm through with philosophy," answered Leander. He gave a bitter laugh. " 'How shall I live?'—what a useless question. That, and a gold aureus, will buy me passage to Alexandria."

I felt such tenderness for Leander. I no longer wished to be alone on an island with him—I only wished him well. "You don't need to stay here reading tragedies unless you want to." I held out a small drawstring bag. "For your third sister's dowry and your voyage back to Alexandria."

Astonished, Leander felt the weight of the gold coins in the bag. "I shouldn't accept—"

"Please," I insisted. "You've been a good friend to me. It would make me glad to think of you in Alexandria. I don't think you should give up philosophy. This is how I think *you* should live: I think you should go back to Alexandria and teach philosophy."

Leander bowed deeply. He struggled to say something. Finally he muttered, "My heartfelt thanks."

Leander left the next day with a caravan headed for Egypt. I missed him badly, and I fidgeted around the palace, feeling sorry for myself. So this was what I got for repenting— I'd lost my only friend in Tiberias. I tried to distract myself with a new project: arranging for girls' classes at the shrine to Diana.

Whether that indecent picture of me hurt or helped, Philip arrived at the palace five days after Leander left. The weather was warm as usual, but I shivered as I went to meet him in the smaller garden. I was hardly aware of Gundi, humming a triumphant Freya-Aphrodite hymn behind me.

There stood Philip, looking very serious. I wanted to run right out of the garden, but I forced myself to approach him and greet him. I wondered how I could have been so determined, on his last visit, to ignore him and to rush back to Rome.

"I was afraid you wouldn't come," I said. "I was afraid you wouldn't want a wife who had disgraced herself in front of the whole court."

"It crossed my mind," admitted Philip. "But then I thought, I am a Herod, son of King Herod, called the Great. I can do whatever I want!"

I smiled weakly. I'd never expected to hear Philip make that joke.

"You explained yourself in your letter," Philip continued soberly, "and now I will explain where I stand. I left Tiberias fearing that you were your mother's daughter, as cruel as you were beautiful. Your letter told of a different Salome, and I had to come back to see for myself. I wanted to look into your eyes and hear it from your lips."

I felt as naked as the night I'd danced at the banquet. In front of Philip, I was a foolish, selfish girl who'd helped to murder an innocent man. I wanted to cover my face, but I kept my hands at my sides and raised my eyes to Philip's. "It's as I wrote in my letter," I said. "I want to turn my life around."

"And I want to believe you," he said. His eyes searched

my face with an intimate, yearning gaze, more frightening than Antipas's lecherous stare had been. I trembled like a criminal before a judge, awaiting my sentence.

"Salome," said Philip tenderly. Taking my hand, he kissed the palm. "Let's begin a new life together."

I thought I was going to give a shout of joy, but instead I started to cry. I blubbered that it was only because I was so grateful and happy. That was true, but I was also crying because I was sad and ashamed.

"Come, come," said Philip, kissing my wet eyelids. "Enough sorrow! I'll put my seal on the marriage contract, and then we have an unpleasant task before us: we must celebrate our wedding with Antipas and Herodias."

Philip was right about the unpleasantness. To start with, I hated giving Herodias the satisfaction of doing what she wanted. She talked as if she'd personally arranged the match with Philip from the beginning. "And isn't it a stroke of good luck that Agrippa arrived in time for your wedding!"

I'd never liked my uncle Agrippa, Herodias's brother. His arrival, to take the position of market master in Tiberias, gave me another reason to leave.

Herodias wanted to plan an extravagant wedding feast, and of course she wouldn't listen to me. I begged Philip to insist on a quiet celebration, one that could take place within a day or so. And one that could be held in the small dining hall off the main garden. How could Herodias even *think* of holding another banquet in the hall where . . . ?

To me, Herodias's ability to gloss over that hideous evening was not quite sane. Or was it only a normal trait for a Herod? In any case, if Philip and I had children, I hoped the strain wouldn't come out in them.

Herodias would have liked to spend weeks (and bags of Antipas's gold) shopping for my trousseau. But she did the best she could on one market day in Tiberias. I was well supplied with fine linens and silks, costly ointments, a mirror of my own, and all the other accessories a tetrarch's wife might need. Herodias wanted to buy a trained lady's maid for me, too, but I asked to keep Gundi instead. She was a self-serving old thing, but I was fond of her anyway. Besides, I'd promised.

Magus Shazzar drew up a joint horoscope for Philip and me. Surprisingly, he pronounced the next day very favorable for our wedding. And the day after that, the stars indicated, was favorable for a journey across the water. Imagine!

The wedding feast was held in the smaller dining hall, as I wished. But even so, Herodias and Antipas managed a showy celebration. For entertainment, there were acrobats and trained monkeys (although no dancers) as well as musicians. Antipas's famous cook outdid himself, producing three new dishes. Herodias wore her stunning blond wig. Antipas got drunk and joked loudly with Uncle Agrippa about how he and Philip had both married scorpions, mother and daughter. Herodias slapped him playfully.

I'd thought I'd closed my mind to anything my step-father might say, but his words scraped like sand on a half-healed wound. As Uncle Agrippa added his own crude joke about how to mate with a female scorpion, I turned shakily to Philip. Philip was already on his feet, his face stony. Pulling me up from our dining couch, he made some excuse, and we left the hall.

Crossing the smaller garden to the guest suite, I sobbed, "I don't want to be a scorpion. Please . . ."

I didn't know exactly what I wanted from Philip, but he paused by the fish pond and took my face in his hands. "Salome, listen. Here's what I'm going to do for tonight. I'm declaring the guest suite a territory under the protection of Gaulanitis. We'll spend the night there, safe from the evil vapors of this place. And then in the morning, we'll be gone."

I sniffled and gave a deep sigh. "Yes! I'll jump onto the royal barge—the right barge this time." Philip gave me a quizzical look. I'd explain to him later. "Anyway, I'll stop crying now, I promise."

The next day, the household gathered on the docks to wish Philip and me goodbye, good health, and long life. I thought of my two missing friends, Joanna and Leander. Philip's barge pushed off from the docks, headed for the eastern shore of Lake Tiberias. The Tetrarch of Galilee and Perea and his wife, wearing their official purple robes, waved farewell to us from under an awning. I watched them shrink to two purple dots.

While Philip went forward to talk to the captain, I turned away from Antipas's city. Shading my eyes, I gazed at the highlands on the far side of the lake. It would be good to leave the moist, thick climate of Tiberias, I thought, and get up into the hills. And I was eager to see the woodland shrine that Philip had told me about.

Out of the corner of my eye, I caught sight of something yellow. For one eerie heartbeat, I thought Herodias had materialized right behind me. I screamed loud enough to bring Philip running from the other end of the barge.

And then I began to laugh. What I'd seen was indeed Herodias's blond wig. But the face under the blond hair wasn't my mother's. It was a broad, red face.

"Gundi! You took your hair back."

The stolen wig, still elaborately arranged as Herodias had worn it last night, didn't quite cover Gundi's gray hair. But Gundi looked as pleased as if she were the one who'd married a tetrarch. Her blue eyes almost disappeared in the crinkles of her smile.

# AFTERWORD

Salome, daughter of Herodias, great-granddaughter of Herod the Great, was an actual historical person, but very few facts are known about her. One of those facts, sadly, is that Salome's husband, Philip, died only a few years after they married. They had no children. The Roman Emperor—now Caligula—gave Philip's territory to Salome's uncle Agrippa. Salome married again, to another relative, Aristobolus of Chalcis in Syria. Her face in profile can be seen on a coin issued by Aristobolus.

As for Herod Antipas and Herodias, they were finally punished, in a roundabout way. The Nabatean king, angry with Antipas for rejecting his daughter, attacked Perea. He defeated Antipas's troops and took some territory away from him. Since that territory actually belonged to the Roman Empire, the powers in Rome were not pleased with Antipas.

In AD 37, the Emperor Tiberius died, and Caligula inherited the throne. Herodias (apparently not understanding how disappointed the Imperial government was in her husband) urged Antipas to ask the new Emperor to make him king of all Judea. Instead, the Emperor decided to banish Antipas and Herodias to Gaul.

Caligula also appointed Agrippa, Herodias's brother, as

ruler of Herod the Great's former kingdom of Greater Judea. Agrippa eventually died a horrible death in Caesarea, "eaten by worms," as the Book of Acts puts it.

All my quotations from the Bible follow the Revised Standard Version, 1977, published by Oxford University Press, Inc.